Through the Fire

MYSTERY
and the
MINISTER'S
WIFE™

Through the Fire

DIANE NOBLE

GUIDEPOSTS BOOKS
CARMEL, NEW YORK

www.guideposts.org
(800) 431-2344
Guideposts Books & Inspirational Media Division

Cover design by Dugan Design Group
Cover illustration by Rose Lowry, www.illustrations.com
Interior design by Cris Kossow
Typeset by Nancy Tardi
Printed in the United States of America

To all my friends at Trinity Oaks in Salisbury, North Carolina—
you are an inspiration!

Chapter One

K ate Hanlon smoothed her skirt, straightened the buttons on her periwinkle cardigan, and adjusted the silver drop-pendant at her neck. With a sigh, she flipped down the visor mirror and fussed with her strawberry-blonde collar-length hair in an attempt to tame the frizz brought on by the mist outside the car. Then she sighed again.

Her husband, Paul, who was driving Kate's Honda Accord, grinned. "I can tell how close to Copper Mill we're getting by how often you do that."

"The sighing or the primping?"

He laughed. "Both."

"As my mother used to say, you never get a second chance to make a good first impression."

On either side of the narrow road, thick stands of hicko-ries, hemlocks, ashes, and maples were just beginning to turn vibrant oranges, reds, and browns. Since dawn, when they first turned off the main highway into the hill country, a light fog had wrapped itself around the trees, causing the leaves to drip and the scent of damp, loamy soil to drift into the car.

They had been on the road for three days, taking turns at the wheel since leaving San Antonio. The moving van left before they did, and if everything worked according to plan, it would be awaiting them at the new parsonage. Paul's car would arrive a week or so later.

They had hired a couple of college students from Riverbend Community, their former church, to drive Paul's beloved old Lexus Sports Coupe to Tennessee. The boys planned to arrive soon after Paul and Kate did, though Kate worried they might have too much fun on their drive east to make it a hurried trip.

"There's the sign," Paul announced, breaking into her thoughts. He leaned forward, squinting. "Copper Mill, eleven miles. We're almost there, Kate."

He slowed the Accord and turned right onto a single-lane road. Within minutes they were traversing a series of switchbacks as they neared the summit.

The fog turned into gossamer strands as they climbed, then separated into random, thin patches as the sunlight finally broke through. Paul braked as they came to a series of steep curves along the top of the ridge.

They reached a clearing, and Kate sat forward for a better look. The view was breathtaking. Below the summit, ribbons of mist laced in and out among the hollows and ridges. Meandering streams caught the light of the morning sun, turning them into silver threads that almost appeared to be stitched along patches of forest. In the distance, rolling hills folded one behind the other like pale lavender-blue petals until they disappeared into the horizon.

"Oh, Paul! It's beautiful."

But it was the wide valley framed by the hills that caught her attention. Near its northern end was a small town with tree-lined streets and neat rows of houses laid out as if by a giant hand.

"That must be Copper Mill." She studied an area that appeared to be near the creek just outside town, then leaned forward, trying to get a better look. "And it must be fireplace weather."

"Why is that?"

"I see a small wisp of smoke."

The idea of curling up in front of a fireplace in the early autumn chill pleased her. But the image was fleeting. Her thoughts turned again to her concerns about their move, especially to their new church, Faith Briar, and the families who awaited their arrival.

She must have sighed again, because Paul asked, "Are you nervous, Katie?"

She laughed lightly. "Aren't you?"

He glanced at her and grinned. His expression reminded her of their children on the night before Christmas when they were young. She laughed again. "I guess I'll be the one to do the worrying for us both."

They had taken a huge leap of faith when they decided to leave their former church and make the trek from Texas to Tennessee to take on the pastorate of Faith Briar, a small church in a small village nestled in the mountains.

Kate settled back, pulled her feet comfortably onto the seat, and turned toward her husband.

Paul had built the congregation in San Antonio from fewer than one hundred to a membership of more than five thousand, with three Sunday services and a weekly televised program. In their first five years at Riverbend, they had moved from a storefront church to an imposing building that could seat twenty-five hundred in each service. And now Paul was taking over a church that was smaller than most Sunday-school classes in their former church. How could it possibly be enough of a challenge for this dynamic leader? Kate had also given up her job as an executive assistant—without a career of her own, would she find enough to keep her from getting bored?

Kate's thoughts were interrupted when Paul maneuvered the car to the shoulder to let a black-and-white SUV pass. She noticed the sheriff's symbol on the side of the vehicle as it sped past them. The driver was a very young-looking redheaded man in a khaki shirt. The emergency lights on top of the SUV weren't flashing, but the vehicle seemed to be in a hurry and soon disappeared around the next curve.

"I can't wait to see what's ahead." Paul steered the Honda back onto the road. "It's almost as if we're starting over again —like when we were a couple of kids fresh out of seminary." He grinned.

"The closer we get to Copper Mill, the more I realize how scary this is. It's one thing to be committed to following God's leading; it's quite another to take those first wobbly steps into the unknown with confidence and enthusiasm."

"It's only natural . . ."

Laughing, she finished his sentence as long-married couples often did. ". . . after all this anticipation and preparation."

He braked at a hairpin curve as they started the steep decline into the valley, and she tried to picture their new home. Maybe it was a Cape Cod. Or a Victorian. Paul, who didn't pay attention to such things as house exteriors, couldn't tell her. Though it had been just a formality, Paul had flown to Chattanooga, rented a car, and driven to Copper Mill six months earlier. The church board had met with him and extended a warm invitation. He had toured the church, the town, and the parsonage, though he admitted it was dark by the time they reached the last stop on his tour.

He'd told her the house was small. Very small. And a bit dog-eared. "It just needs your decorating touches," he'd said. "And maybe a fresh coat of paint."

Small was okay with Kate. Small could be cottage-cute and lovely.

They came to a clearing in the trees, and Kate noticed that they were closer now, and the details of the town were clearer.

She leaned forward for a better look, her attention riveted to an area just outside town. "Paul!" Her heart did a staccato beat.

He gave her a worried glance. "What is it?"

"That smoke we saw a while back?"

"What about it?"

"It's not from a fireplace. The plume is huge. It looks like a building's on fire!"

Paul picked up speed, looking for a turnout to pull over. Kate tried to catch a glimpse of the fire in the clearings between the stands of hemlocks and maples. Finally, a longer stretch of open sky gave her enough time to stare at the billowing cloud of smoke.

"There's so much smoke, I can't tell where it's coming from."

"Could it be a factory or something? Maybe it's steam from a processing plant?"

"No, it's too dark. Too big. It's a fire, Paul. And now I see an orange glow in the smoke."

Her heart dropped as the sounds of sirens came up suddenly behind them. Paul immediately braked and maneuvered the Accord onto a narrow shoulder.

Sirens blasting and lights flashing, two fire trucks sped by, followed by a large EMS van. The wail of sirens faded into the distance as the vehicles made their way down the switchbacks toward Copper Mill.

"They must be from Pine Ridge," Paul said. "I know Copper Mill has a volunteer fire department, but when they need help, they call on Pine Ridge."

Kate nodded, recognizing the name of the larger town they had passed on their way to Copper Mill.

Through the trees, Kate could see thick black smoke rising from somewhere just outside town. Sick at heart, she turned away as Paul steered the Honda back onto the road, tires spinning gravel and dirt. He picked up speed and raced down the mountain, rounding the corners, tires squealing. Within minutes he closed the gap between the Accord and the emergency vehicles and followed them toward Copper Mill.

Kate held on to the seat, knowing her husband's pastoral heart: he would let nothing get in the way of reaching those in need of help.

The fire trucks slowed and turned onto Mountain Laurel Road, which ran parallel to a creek. Up ahead, flames leaped into the sky above the orange-red smoke.

Before the trucks had even come to a stop at the burning

building, the firefighters had already jumped to the ground. One immediately directed traffic away from the fire and waved Paul and Kate down Smoky Mountain Road.

As Paul inched the car into the smoke and ashes, Kate coughed, her throat stinging and her eyes watering. The stench of wet smoldering embers and acrid smoke drifted toward them.

"I hope no one's hurt," Paul said, his voice low. He drove down a couple of side streets and reconnected with Mountain Laurel Road. Turning right, he headed back toward the densest smoke. The burning building was just outside downtown Copper Mill on a lush tree-lined street.

"There, up ahead! I see people . . . Look, Paul! It's right in front of us."

He hurriedly parked, and they jumped out of the car, grabbing their jackets before slamming the doors. They ran up the sidewalk to where dozens of people stood, young and old, alone and in groups, horror and disbelief showing on their faces.

Paul suddenly stopped, looked at Kate, and then to the burning building. "Oh, Kate."

Kate squinted through the smoke. Flames had almost swallowed the building, but above the uppermost tongues of the roaring fire rose a steeple. Delicate. Fragile. Vulnerable. About to be engulfed in the inferno.

Her eyes watered, but this time it wasn't from the smoke.

The official letter from the church board asking Paul to consider a call to pastor Faith Briar had been written on church stationery. A photograph of the beautiful old church had graced the upper left-hand corner. The steeple was distinctive, its historic bell proudly described below the picture in a paragraph relating the church's history.

Kate's knees went limp, and she grabbed Paul's arm to steady herself.

"No, it can't be," she whispered. "It can't be our church!"

Chapter Two

It's Faith Briar," Paul said. His tone was filled with a sadness Kate knew reached deep into his heart. She followed his gaze to the top of the steeple as it became completely engulfed in flames.

A loud crack was followed by a dull clanging thud as both steeple and bell toppled.

Around Paul and Kate rose cries, deep and sorrowful, almost as if a death had just occurred.

Kate took Paul's hand and squeezed it. After meeting her gaze briefly, he took a deep breath, then turned to the people standing around them.

"Please, I need your attention for a moment," he said, raising his voice to be heard above the cacophony of spraying water and the shouts of the firefighters. "Are any of you part of the Faith Briar congregation?"

Slowly, people turned toward them. At first they frowned, then a slow dawning of recognition showed on a few faces.

An older man with a thin, wiry build moved slowly toward Paul and Kate. "You're our new pastor," he said, leaning on a walking stick. He was bald except for a fringe of white hair above his ears. "I met you when you flew out to look us over."

Paul reached out to shake his hand. "Yes, I remember. It's good to see you again." He turned to Kate. "And this is my wife, Kate."

"Name's Joe Tucker," he said. "Welcome to Copper Mill." He cleared his throat, his eyes watering, and turned to look at the still-flaming building. Others had gathered round now, and everyone seemed to be talking at once.

Joe held up his walking stick to get their attention. "If you didn't get to meet him before, let me introduce the man God knew we would need at this very hour." He gestured to Paul, then turned back to the clusters of parishioners standing nearby. "This is our new shepherd," he said, blinking rapidly, "though it seems his flock is in great need of a—" He choked up and couldn't finish.

Paul stepped up and patted Joe on the back. "Folks, no matter how dark this day seems, God is with us."

"But we've lost everything! I mean, look at it. There's nothing left." A petite middle-aged woman shook her head slowly. A man standing next to her circled his arm around her shoulders. Two teenage boys—one looking big enough to play pro football—stood nearby, staring at the scene across the street, seeming too stunned to speak.

A man who appeared to be in his early thirties was standing a few feet away from Kate. He stared at the fire in disbelief, tears visible behind thick eyeglasses that magnified his eyes. He was trembling. "What will we do?" he said, then his voice dropped to a whisper. "This church . . . not this beautiful little church."

"I can tell you what we'll do," another woman said. Even though she appeared to be in her early seventies, she was wearing heels and a faux leopard-skin coat. She cuddled a tiny bug-eyed Chihuahua in her arms, keeping her chin high and her shoulders back, as if taking personal charge of the tragedy's aftermath. She glanced at Paul and Kate briefly, almost as if they didn't matter, then turned back to the gathering crowd. "As a member of the church board, I say we march right over to the fire captain and ask how this could have happened."

"This is not the ti—" Paul began.

She shushed him and kept talking, raising her voice even louder. "We need to find out why this happened and place the blame where the blame belongs. We need to examine the evidence, find out who saw the fire break out, and if they noticed anyone suspicious around."

This time Paul spoke more forcefully. "There's no need for that right now. The fire department will look into it, I'm sure. And local authorities—the sheriff and his staff—will launch their own investigation."

The woman dismissed Paul's words with a flutter of her French-manicured fingernails and, high heels clicking, started toward the fire chief near one of the trucks. "Yoo-hoo," she called out as she sidestepped puddles and stretched-out hoses. "Yoo-hoo . . ."

"You'll have to forgive her," Joe Tucker said. "She sometimes acts as if Faith Briar belongs to no one but her. She has a good heart, but . . ." he began, then obviously thought better of what he was about to say. "Her name's Renee Lambert." He smiled as if he might actually be fond of the woman. "And her mutt's name is Kisses. She never goes anywhere without him."

The petite woman who had spoken earlier smiled at Kate and Paul. "This wasn't the welcome we'd planned." She looked across the street at the clouds of smoke. "We were going to have a luncheon for you in the fellowship hall tomorrow."

Then she smiled suddenly and reached out her hand to Kate. "I'm afraid this has made us all forget our manners. My name is Livvy Jenner." She glanced over her shoulder. "And this is my husband, Danny. Our sons, Justin and James. We're members of Faith Briar . . ." Her voice caught. "I'm sorry. It's just that this church means everything to us . . ."—she gestured to the silent parishioners around her—"to us all. To those of us raised in Copper Mill, and that's most of us here, it's the only church we've ever known. Danny and I were married in this church. He's on the church board, and I work in the nursery on Sunday mornings. And now . . . this."

Kate squeezed Livvy's hand. How could she find the words that would comfort her? In a time like this, words were inadequate. Finally, she said simply, "We've come to help, to do everything we can."

By now the word had spread that Paul and Kate had arrived, and several more people joined the earlier group to meet them. After they had been introduced around once more, Paul stepped forward and raised his voice so all could hear.

"There is a passage in Isaiah 61 that seems appropriate on this dark day. I think it might bring us comfort to hear it." He pulled his pocket Bible from his jacket and opened it. The crowd fell silent, except for a few sounds of soft weeping.

"To all who mourn in Israel, he will give beauty for ashes, joy instead of mourning, praise instead of despair. For the LORD has planted them like strong and graceful oaks for his own glory."

Compassion filled Paul's clear blue eyes as he gazed at the despairing crowd in front of him.

"We mourn today, my friends," he said. "But God's promise is this: The ashes you see now will someday be exchanged for something of exquisite beauty, your mourning exchanged for joy beyond measure. That is our hope—he is our hope, and we must cling to his promises. We don't know how it will happen, or even when . . . but consider this: God has planted you like strong and graceful oaks here in this place. He will give you the strength, the stamina, to get through this tragedy."

By now the firefighters had subdued the worst of the flames, but all that was left was a charred, burnt-out hulk of a building and a wet, smoldering pile of ashes and embers.

"And I can tell you this," Paul continued. "Faith Briar couldn't be more loved—by you or by our Lord."

As Paul spoke, Kate noticed a middle-aged man sidling closer as if to hear better. By the cast of his shoulders, he seemed broken down by life. His grayish brown hair was thin and collar length. He wore a brown wool plaid shirt, the collar turned up as if to protect his neck from the cold. He met her eyes briefly before turning away. There was something in his expression that haunted her.

She turned her attention back to Paul, whose voice was filled with both sorrow and love for his new flock. "Keep these words in your heart, dear friends. In the dark days ahead, remember: God will give you beauty for ashes, and the oil of joy instead of mourning. We need to remember this promise even as—"

Renee Lambert hollered "Yoo-hoo," interrupting him as she started back across the street in her high heels, clutching the Chihuahua. "Listen up, everyone," she cried. "I was right."

Murmurs rose in the crowd as Renee clicked her heels closer, skirting the puddles again before stepping up onto the curb. The Chihuahua's big eyes looked soulful, his oversized ears flopping with each of Renee's tottering steps.

Kate exchanged a quizzical glance with Paul.

"I just heard it from Deputy Spencer himself—" Renee said, then she interrupted herself, staring solemnly at the smoldering ashes. "Our bell . . ." she choked, clutching her hand to her bosom. "Our beautiful historic bell . . . it's covered in mud and debris." She looked up at the crowd helplessly. "I have a special place in my heart for the old thing . . ."

"We all do," Danny Jenner said, his voice raspy with emotion. "We all do. And I promise you, we'll keep it safe. We can't lose the bell too."

Renee nodded.

"Renee," Livvy said. "You were about to tell us something?"

Renee brightened considerably. "Oh yes. My news," she said with a dramatic sigh. "I heard it from the deputy himself: It's arson!"

Chapter Three

The next morning, Kate rose at five thirty and tiptoed from the bedroom, being careful not to wake Paul.

She padded toward the kitchen to make coffee. But when she reached the living room, she stopped. "Oh boy," she breathed and fell into the nearest chair—the only one without a stack of boxes.

Of all the strange rooms in this tiny, sixties ranch-style house, the living room was the strangest. For one thing, it was as big as a barn. The rest of the entire parsonage could probably fit in it with room to spare.

A river-rock fireplace took up one corner of the room. Two walls were covered with fake walnut paneling that absorbed the light, and a third was made up of sliding-glass doors that were so covered with hard-water deposits, they were nearly opaque. The ceiling lights consisted of plastic-covered fluorescent tubes, which attacked Kate's artistic senses every time she flipped the switch.

As she sat here now, she decided that if she were to design the homeliest living room on the planet, this would be the decor she would choose. From fake wood paneling to moss green shag carpeting. The opaque sliders were a nice touch as well.

She looked up at the fluorescent lighting set against a ceiling covered with acoustic popcorn coating. It was a decorator's worst nightmare. She started to giggle. "Oh, Lord! You do have a sense of humor."

The whole house was a nightmare, each room more garish than the previous one. Her personal favorite was the guest bathroom, with its wallpaper of silver foil, a trellis of orange and yellow, and a wild sprinkling of nine-inch poppies in various shades of peach, mauve, and moss green.

Still giggling, she stood and headed to the kitchen.

When she and Paul lived in San Antonio, every morning she rose before sunup, fixed a large mug of fresh-ground coffee, and sat in her favorite rocking chair near an east-facing window that let in the early morning sunlight. Starting her day in the quiet dawn with meditation, prayer, and a chapter from the Psalms saw her through whatever troubles—or joys—that might come her way.

But this morning she had the sinking feeling it would take a miracle to find the coffeemaker. Or a mug. Or the coffee beans. Or the grinder. And honestly, she was in no mood to pray.

She rummaged through two boxes, which, though marked quite clearly, didn't contain anything close to what she was looking for. Then she tried another large box the movers had left on the stove.

On the stove? What were they thinking? The box was so

heavy, she couldn't make it budge, let alone move it to the floor so she could use the stovetop.

She leaned against the kitchen counter and surveyed her small domain. Boxes were stacked three high and so close together they covered the kitchen floor. What she could see of the faded yellow cupboards was smudged with fingerprints.

There was no doubt that she could handle the scrubbing, mopping, and scouring, but it was the size of the rooms, with the exception of the living room, that had her stymied. She adored gourmet cooking, and her heart sank to her knees as she looked around the kitchen, taking in its too-few cupboards, its twenty-five-year-old refrigerator that rattled and whirred like it was ready to fly to the moon, and its stove that—before the box was placed on the stovetop—she had noticed appeared of an age to have been delivered by mule and buggy in the early years of Copper Mill.

She felt a headache coming on just thinking about the work ahead. She needed coffee, and fast.

She plowed through another cardboard box, a smaller one she vaguely remembered packing at the last minute. Stacked at the top were table linens and napkins, different matching sets from Williams-Sonoma. Then, finally, at the bottom of the box, she found the grinder and the coffee beans. It took a few more tries to find the mugs and coffeemaker. The coffee filters were missing completely, so she put a paper towel in the basket, ground the beans, flipped the switch, and hoped for the best.

When the last drip had landed in the carafe, Kate poured

herself a fresh mug of coffee, then returned to the living room
with her Bible. The furniture that wouldn't fit in the other
rooms was jammed against the walls, with stacks of boxes
between, spilling out into the center of the room. Even her
little spinet piano was stacked with unpacked boxes. She settled again into the rocking chair and took a sip of coffee.

"How can I stand this?" she whispered, a halfhearted
prayerful plea that she was certain bounced back from the
popcorn ceiling. She looked down at the Bible resting in her
lap but didn't have the energy to open it. Instead, her mind
whirled with the work that lay ahead just to get the parsonage in a livable condition, sans fingerprint smudges, dust
bunnies, and soiled cupboards. She leaned her head against
the high-back rocker and closed her eyes.

How could she even think about praying when her mind
was filled with so much to do? She'd left her beautiful home
in San Antonio for this?

Then her eyes flew open. What was she thinking?

Here she was, focused on herself, when the congregation
they had been called to serve had just suffered a devastating
loss. Here she was, complaining about the parsonage decor,
without considering that an elderly and saintly man, Paul's
mentor, had lived here alone, and probably lonely, for two
decades after his wife died.

Kate was ashamed. And humbled.

"Oh, Lord, forgive me," she whispered. Then she bowed
her head and prayed for the Faith Briar congregation, their
heartaches and fears, and she prayed for Nehemiah Jacobs,
the seventy-nine-year-old former pastor of Faith Briar, who
had recommended Paul for the position. He had moved to an

assisted-living facility in Chattanooga. She wondered if he was comfortable there, or if he was as dismayed by his new life as she was by hers. She prayed for God's peace to envelop him; she prayed for the hurting families, the young, the elderly, all the members of Faith Briar's congregation, that God would heal their heartaches and give them wisdom for the days ahead; she prayed for Paul, that God would strengthen him for the task of building up the brokenhearted and rebuilding the church.

Finally, she prayed for herself, asking simply that God would make her acutely aware of seeing the world through his eyes, with his heart of compassion.

She looked up after her prayer and again took in the room. Somehow it didn't seem quite as grim as before. The sunlight was valiantly trying to shine through the milky sliding-glass doors. She walked across the room, opened the slider, and stepped outside. Sunlight filtered through the branches of the maple tree, creating a dappled pattern on the overgrown lawn. Beads of dew reflected the light, looking like a thousand tiny jewels had been cast across the yard during the night.

It didn't matter that the weeds had grown tall in the postage-stamp-sized backyard or that the rosebushes were half dead. It didn't matter that she could still smell ashes in the air. It didn't matter, because if she looked beyond the ordinary she might see something of beauty.

Paul's words came back to her: Out of the ashes would come beauty. Mourning would be exchanged for the oil of joy.

"Yes!" she exclaimed and punched the air the way her kids used to. "Yes!"

"Yes?" came the sleepy voice behind her.

She turned and laughed and stepped back inside. Paul was scuffing across the shag carpet in slippered feet, his hair mussed, his bathrobe half-tied. He scanned the room, his expression probably much like hers had been. With a sigh he moved a stack of boxes and sat down on the piano bench.

"So it wasn't a nightmare," he said with a half smile.

"This room?"

He nodded. "I've never seen anything quite like it."

She laughed. "I've come up with a plan. We can make this house work."

He quirked a brow. "You've always been creative, but this . . . ?" He rolled his eyes at the popcorn ceiling, then shot her a mischievous grin.

"I'll figure out how to scrape it off. It can't be that hard." She sat down on a cardboard box across from him. "Besides, a house doesn't need to be large to be welcoming and warm."

He nodded. "I couldn't agree more."

"We'll need to get rid of about half of our furniture."

"Can you let your antiques go?"

The little twist of her heart lasted only a moment. She nodded. "Yes. Plus a lot of other things. We've talked about simplifying our lives. It's time to do it with a clean sweep."

"I agree, but it may be harder than you think. What about your Mauviel?"

She grinned at him. "I scrimped and saved for years to buy that copperware. I can't let it go now. That's where I put my foot down."

"But the cupboards here . . ."

"Too small, I know." She stood to go to the kitchen to get Paul some coffee. Stopping at the doorway between the two rooms, she looked back and said, "I've already figured that out." She eyed the ceiling above the breakfast bar.

"The ceiling?" Paul said.

"I just thought of it. I'll hang all those gorgeous pots and pans from hooks."

"Are you sure? The kitchen is so small."

"It's a European thing. I've seen pictures."

Paul reached for his mug. "Honey, all this means a lot to me," he said.

She sipped her coffee, waiting for him to go on.

"What you're doing—how you're being so, well, creative and wonderful about this. I know this isn't easy for you, leaving San Antonio, leaving friends and relatives you love, moving to a place where everything is new and different. And this . . ."—he looked around the room, shaking his head—"this can't be easy. You've always taken such pride in your decorating skills, your artistic sense of things, your ability to entertain with a gourmet touch."

She started to speak, but he held up his hand. "Before you say anything, I just want you to know that once in a while I see a fleeting expression on your face." He paused, his expression gentle. "It tells me you're sad when you think of home."

She moved closer to him and took his hands in hers. "This is home, Paul. Home is where you are."

His voice was gruff when he continued. "I love you, Katie, for your willingness to give up so much to come here. I just wanted you to know."

She smiled at him, her heart swelling with love for this man. "All I need is time to get this place in order. I would die of embarrassment if anyone came in for a visit before we've at least got our furniture arranged and unpacked a few dozen boxes."

Before Paul could respond, the doorbell rang. He frowned. "It's a bit early for visitors. What time is it? Seven?"

She stood, put down her mug, and retied her robe before heading to the door. "Maybe it's an emergency." The phone line wouldn't be activated until the following week, so the only way anyone could contact them was to stop by.

She opened the door and peered out.

The blonde woman who had been wearing the faux leopard-skin coat the day before was standing on the front porch, her little Chihuahua in her arms. Today she was dressed in a velveteen warm-up suit. She was wearing full makeup, and her blonde hair was swept up into a fancy do. Silver earrings dangled from her ears, sparkling in the morning sunlight. "Hello—it's Renee, isn't it?" Kate said.

"Renee Lambert," the woman said and swept into the room without invitation. A cloud of Estée Lauder's Youth-Dew wafted in behind her.

"Please, come in," Kate said to Renee's back as she disappeared into the living room.

"Oh, Pastor Paul," the woman gushed. "I'm so sorry we didn't get properly reintroduced yesterday. I did meet you when we hired you, as you probably remember. I'm a member of the church board."

Paul stood, looking as if he wanted to be swallowed up by the moss green shag carpet—robe, pajamas, spiked hair, and all. "Yes, of course. But if you'll excuse me, I was just about to get dressed." He hurried from the room and disappeared into the master bedroom.

Renee helped herself to the rocking chair, pulling the nervous Chihuahua onto her lap. "While we're waiting for your husband, I'll take some tea, if you would be so kind."

"I have coffee made," Kate said sweetly, "but the tea will have to wait. I'm afraid the stove is out of commission right now, even if I could find the kettle and tea bags."

Renee fluttered her fingers. "I don't drink coffee," she said. "I think dependency on caffeine is a sign of a weak constitution. As for tea, I wouldn't let a paper tea bag near my hot water. I prefer loose leaf. Though in a pinch I've been known to dunk a tea bag made of silk."

"*Hmm . . .*" was the only response Kate could manage. Seated again on the cardboard box, she reached for her mug and took a sip of coffee. A nice long sip to bolster her constitution.

Paul returned, gave Renee a warm smile, then sat down again on the piano bench. "Now, how can we help you?"

She fluttered her fingers again. Her long, squared-off nails appeared to be acrylic, painted in French manicure pale pink and white. "Actually, Pastor. It's what you two can do for us."

Paul gave her another smile, though Kate noticed it was getting a little tight. "We're here to serve, Renee."

"Tomorrow's Sunday, as you know. And our congregation doesn't have anyplace to meet."

"I'm aware of that. Last night I spoke to—"

"You see, back in '87 when the flood hit, we had to find another meeting place. Then in '95, little Sydney Hill flushed her rubber duck down the toilet, backing up the plumbing, and in '97, we had a freak snowstorm. It broke the water pipes and ruined the heating system." She sat back, looking smug.

Kate wondered where Renee was going with this. From the look on Paul's face, he did too.

"You see," Renee continued, patting the Chihuahua's head, "whenever these sorts of things hit our little church, it's up to the pastor to provide a place to meet."

"I'm aware of that," Paul began again. "That's why—"

"As in *here*," she finished with a gesture that took in the entire living room. "It's up to the pastor," she said, turning to Kate, "and in this case, his wife, to have the congregation meet . . . *here*."

The light dawned, and Kate sat back utterly shocked. "Here?" she squeaked.

"Didn't you wonder why the room is so large?" Renee rushed on without waiting for an answer. "We added on after the flood of '87, just in case it ever happened again."

Kate swallowed hard and waited for Paul to tell Renee it was impossible. She glanced around the room at the stacks of boxes, the furniture crammed into every square inch of space, and her heart fell. She wasn't a neat freak, but she did at least require comfortable places for people to sit down. Preferably, not on top of boxes.

"Renee," she began, keeping her voice calm. "Really, we can't—" She stopped abruptly when she caught Paul's expression.

He was ready to laugh, a merry, gracious laugh. She could see it in his eyes.

Suddenly the whole thing struck her as funny. She bit back her own laugh and turned to Renee. "As I was saying, we can't possibly say no. Of course we'll have services here tomorrow."

"I knew you would understand," Renee said, then took in the room as if for the first time. "But, really, you must do something about all . . . this." She shuddered. "Really."

She put Kisses on the floor, then, leading him on a jeweled leash, started for the door. Just before she stepped through the doorway, she turned. "Did you hear about the arrest?"

They shook their heads.

"A man was seen at the church just after the fire broke out. He was arrested late last night for arson." She lowered her voice and moved closer. "I actually saw him watching the fire from across the street. You might have noticed him. Stringy hair, hateful eyes. My neighbor Lola said he was wearing a brown plaid shirt when he was arrested. She heard it from her sister Maude who heard it from Skip Spencer, the sheriff's deputy. Brown shirt or not, I thought he looked shifty, if you know what I mean."

Chapter Four

The following morning, it was still dark when Kate's eyes flew open. She lay there for a moment, her muscles aching from rearranging furniture and unpacking boxes the day before. Paul was snoring softly beside her. By nature, Kate was a morning person, early to rise to enjoy the first moments of the new day all to herself. She laughingly told others she rose early so she could talk to God before he got busy with everyone else.

But this morning was different. Though she and Paul had worked all day Saturday to try to bring some semblance of order to the little parsonage, she still had a million things to do to get ready for the morning service. There was no time for prayer, or even a cup of coffee. With a sigh, she swung her legs over the side of the bed, grabbed her robe, and padded down the hallway.

But as soon as she flipped on the fluorescent lights in the living room, she groaned and changed her mind. She might have a million things to do, but with her spirits threatening to sag with worry over how she could possibly get everything ready, she decided it was more important than ever to start her day with spiritual sustenance. She reached for her Bible, flipped off the tube lighting, and settled into her favorite rocking chair. It was the only comfortable seat with a table lamp beside it.

Fifteen minutes later, her heart felt pounds lighter. She hurriedly changed into her jeans and an old shirt, and humming one of Paul's favorite old hymns, "When We All Get to Heaven," she again flipped on the overhead lighting, tried not to cringe, and went to work.

By 6:03 she had cleared the spinet piano of Paul's reference books—seven boxes of heavy tomes on theology and philosophy, and at least four different Bible translations—and stacked them in nearby bookcases for Paul to rearrange later.

By 6:47 she had scooted some of the heavier boxes from the center of the room to the sides to make space for seating the congregation. And by 7:32 she had found several stacks of metal folding chairs in the garage, delivered by two men from the First Baptist Church the day before. Ten minutes later, Paul, pajamas and robe still on and hair mussed, padded into the garage with two mugs of coffee.

He handed one to her and, with his opposite hand, pulled a couple of folding chairs together. They sat down in the middle of the room, stacks of boxes rising like a cardboard highrise city around them.

Kate read the concern in her husband's eyes. "We've got a difficult morning ahead of us."

Paul took a sip of coffee, then placing the mug on the floor beside him, leaned forward, forearms resting on his knees, fingers dangling. "The congregation is still in shock.

Once that wears off, the sorrow will come. And maybe anger, especially toward the person who set the fire. Getting through all that is enough of an ordeal. Then there's the cleanup and rebuilding..." He reached for his cup.

"I want to encourage them," he continued after taking a sip of coffee, "give them hope for their future, for our future together." He was watching her intently. "But we're outsiders. I worry they won't want our help because of that. In the middle of the night, I was awake praying for Faith Briar, knowing that today may be the most difficult of Sundays to get through. People will have questions, not just about the fire, but possibly about their faith."

She nodded, putting aside all thought of the dirty windows in the living room, the rust stains in the guest-bath toilet, the cluttered kitchen counter, the cookies she planned to bake for after the service . . . or the fact that it all needed to be done by a quarter to ten. Instead, she smiled and reached for Paul's hand.

"First of all," she said, "you were called to Copper Mill—by this congregation, and by God. No matter what has happened, they'll look to you for leadership. They know you've been involved in building plans before. They'll listen to you. I could see it in their eyes from the moment we arrived.

"Second of all, I suspect it's not just the folks at Faith Briar who need encouragement. I think their shepherd needs a bit of encouragement too."

He gave her a lopsided grin. "I'm not usually a worrier, but this thing . . ."

"You've never faced anything like this before. Your concern seems only natural to me. And I think that's what you're dealing with—concern, not worry. And as you've had to remind me a thousand times, there's nothing wrong with that."

He took a sip from his mug. "I came out here to bolster your spirits, and here you are, lifting mine." He paused, studying her carefully, laugh lines crinkling at the edges of his eyes. "Aha! You must have caught the ear of our Friend this morning before everyone else did."

She laughed. He knew her whimsical humor well. "Yes, I had his full attention earlier than usual." She squeezed Paul's hand. "I once came across a little saying: 'I do not know the master plan, but it's comforting to know the Master has planned it, and I'm included.'"

Paul smiled and reached for her empty mug as he stood. "And we can't hope for anything more encouraging or comforting than that. All of us are included in the master plan yet to unfold."

"Amen," she said as Paul headed back into the house for refills.

A half hour later they had hauled the folding chairs into the house and lined them in rows facing away from the windows—still smudged and milky after an achy-arm scrubbing the day before. When Paul stepped into his small study to put the final touches on his sermon, Kate continued whirling from room to room, straightening, tidying, and minding the baking cookies.

At 9:14 she fell into the rocker to catch her breath before freshening up and dressing for the service.

She almost groaned as she again took in the odd room. She had added a few personal touches—candles and a basket of silk flowers on the piano, a potted ficus tree in the corner, a fire crackling in the fireplace, a table with extra Bibles and hymnals, boxes of tissues scattered about for the tears she was certain would flow on this difficult Sunday morning— but even with all she'd done, the room still looked barren, stark, and anything but holy.

Worst of all, gaping at her from across the room, stood those mineral-stained sliding-glass doors that had resisted every window-cleaning product—from vinegar to straight ammonia—she had tried.

She sat forward, squinting. As the thin autumn sun hit the glass doors, a pattern appeared.

She blinked and squinted again. If she used her imagination, the milky calcium deposits looked like a flock of sheep —little black faces with bells around their necks.

A flock of sheep etched on her window? She read once that someone claimed to have seen an image of Mother Teresa's face in a cinnamon roll, but here Kate was with sheep baaing at her window.

Humor and grace. That was what she needed so clearly this day. She smiled. *Thank you, Lord.*

THE DOORBELL RANG at 9:37.

Standing in the entryway, Paul adjusted his tie and Kate smoothed her hair. They exchanged quick smiles of encouragement and headed for the door to greet the first of their parishioners.

A tall, broad-shouldered man stepped over the threshold and shook hands with them both. "Sam Gorman," he said in a booming voice. Kate liked him immediately. There was something endearing about his ready smile and the awkward way he carried himself. It was as if his body was a ship sailing on too small a sea. Even his tanned face; his thick, brown, windblown hair; and the permanent squint of his ocean-blue eyes reminded Kate of a sea captain from some bygone era.

He glanced down at the hymnal tucked under one arm and gave her a sheepish grin. "Believe it or not, I'm the church organist, though temporarily without an instrument. I don't suppose you might have a spare?"

Kate laughed. "I've got a small piano—a spinet. But it's terribly out of tune, especially after the move. I tried playing it yesterday, and the sound was awful."

"Lead me to it," he said, looking as if an out-of-tune piano was the least of his worries. She noticed his hands were too bulky and wide for a musician's, which made her wonder what his playing might be like.

She showed Sam the living room, and without hesitation, he pushed back the piano bench, set his music on the built-in stand, and rested his fingers on the keys for a moment without moving. Kate thought he might be praying.

Not wanting to disturb him, she tiptoed from the room. Before she had reached the entryway, Sam began to play.

She halted midstep, then turned back to the living room. The big man was almost curled over the keyboard, his hands dancing its length then back again. He played without self-consciousness, and the music that rose from her old, dilapidated piano was like no sound the little instrument had ever made before.

By now, others had arrived and were taking their seats. Many they had met at the fire: Livvy and Danny Jenner and their two teenage sons, Justin and James; Joe Tucker, the backwoodsman who had been the first to greet them; LuAnne Matthews, a waitress at the local diner who had delighted them by dropping by a piping hot lasagna the night before; and Betty Anderson, who introduced herself as the proprietor of Betty's Beauty Parlor.

Quietly, they found their seats, listening gravely as Sam played "On Holy Ground." Still more parishioners poured in, silently, sometimes in couples, sometimes in families, sometimes alone. Even the smallest children seemed subdued.

Kate didn't know how long she stood there, transfixed. She only knew it was a moment she would never forget. The homely room with its fluorescent lighting and shag carpet, its blotchy sliding-glass doors, disappeared.

In its place was a sanctuary. The words she'd read that morning came back to her: "One thing have I desired of the LORD, that will I seek after; that I may dwell in the house of the LORD all the days of my life, to behold the beauty of the LORD."

She blinked back a sting of tears. She was beholding the Lord's beauty this moment, in the faces of his people, who had gathered to worship him, in the music that filled the room.

Paul came to stand beside her as Sam continued playing. *We are standing on holy ground* . . . flooded her mind, her soul. She looked up at her husband and knew he felt it too. "This truly is holy ground," she whispered. "I'm surprised we didn't notice it earlier."

Promptly at 10:00, Danny Jenner, chairman of the Faith Briar church board, smiled and went up to stand in front of the little congregation. He was a tall, slender man with dark, curly hair. His best feature was his smile, which transformed his face from rather ordinary to handsome. He was obviously used to speaking in public and was quite eloquent in his introduction of Paul and Kate, mentioning the great blessings God had in store for them all, no matter the circumstances that shadowed their arrival.

Paul went up to stand beside him, shook his hand, and thanked everyone for coming. As Danny sat down with his wife, Livvy and their teenage sons, Paul asked that the congregation continue in the spirit of worship, holding all questions and comments about the tragic fire until after the service. Kate slipped into the back row as he announced the Scripture reading.

She had just settled back in her chair, preparing her heart for worship, when the front door opened with a bang and the sound of high heels clicking on the slate-floored entry carried toward her. Before Kate could jump up to welcome the late-comer, the telltale waft of Estée Lauder Youth-Dew descended on her, followed by the jostling creak of a folding chair, and a heavy sigh. Kate looked up as Renee Lambert plopped down in a chair next to her.

Kisses, on jeweled leash, hopped onto her lap. "Dear?" Renee said to Kate in a loud whisper, "Would you mind moving down? I don't believe we have enough room."

Kate took the seat to her left. The teacup-sized Chihuahua fixed a soulful gaze on her before scampering onto the seat she had just vacated.

She told herself not to be annoyed and tried to return her attention to Paul. But the little dog seemed transfixed with her, ears at full alert, his tail thumping on the chair, his tiny body shaking. She'd heard somewhere that very small dogs often do that, even when they aren't cold. But if she didn't know better, she would have thought he was purposely looking pitiful so he could sit on her lap. And she guessed that if Renee noticed, there would be no stopping her until Kisses got what Kisses wanted.

She turned slightly away from the dog and crossed her legs.

Paul was speaking of their shared sorrow but also of coming joy. "Weeping may endure for a night," he said, "but the promise God gives us is that joy—his joy—will return in the morning.

"Again and again throughout Scripture, we have his promise that no matter what, he will be with us," he said. "In Isaiah 43, the promise is one that seems written especially for us today: 'Fear not, for I have redeemed you; I have called you by your name; you are mine.

"'When you pass through the waters, I will be with you; and through the rivers, they shall not overflow you. When you walk through the fire you shall not be burned. . . . Fear not, for I am with you.'"

Paul drew his sermon to a close, and Sam began playing "It Is Well with My Soul." He nodded to the congregation to join him, this time singing along. When he reached the chorus, his booming baritone almost shook the windows.

Kate closed her eyes, letting the words soak into her soul. *When peace like a river attendeth my way, when sorrows like sea billows roll . . .*

She felt a tap on her shoulder, and her eyes flew open.

"I need to talk to you . . ." Renee said in a loud whisper, "with you being the minister's wife and all. It's about that arsonist . . . and something I think I remember about him . . ." She raised a thin-penciled brow as if Kate knew what she was talking about. When Kate didn't respond, Renee leaned even closer. "It's something I can't quite put my finger on, but I know it will be instrumental to the investigation."

"Investigation?"

"You know, the man they've arrested?"

Kate nodded. The one Renee mentioned the day before.

"Guilty as dirt, if you ask me. And I intend to see that justice is done. He's familiar. I know I've seen him before, but I just don't remember where . . . I mean, before he drifted into town. Really, we all know he was one step from being homeless, staying in some dirty boarding house across the tracks, if you know what I mean . . ."

Kate held up a hand to stop what was turning into a tirade of gossip.

The hymn had concluded, and Paul was now inviting the congregation to stay for a time of fellowship with cookies, tea, and coffee. He closed in prayer, then Sam played "His Eye Is on the Sparrow." Though it was meant as a postlude, one by one, people joined in, singing softly as they made their way to the table where Kate had earlier set out refreshments.

As the final notes faded, Renee sidled closer, cupping her hand to Kate's ear. "As I was about to say earlier . . ." Her whisper was so loud, people near them craned to look.

Kate flashed Renee a smile and tried to sidle by her. "I'm sorry. I really must run—I need to see to the coffee and tea."

The older woman apparently didn't notice the rebuff,

because she nodded happily as she stepped back to let Kate pass. "Of course, of course! We'll talk later." She scratched Kisses on the head with the tips of her acrylic French-manicured nails. "But don't forget."

TWO HOURS LATER, the meeting was over, and everyone was gone but Livvy and Danny Jenner, whose boys were hauling the folding chairs back to the garage.

Grateful, Kate sank into her rocker as Livvy sat down in an overstuffed chair beside her. Paul and Danny were in the garage, stacking the chairs as the boys brought them.

"Your kids are great."

Livvy laughed. "Don't tell them that." Livvy's hair was short and auburn, the sides tucked behind her ears, which fit her petite frame. She wore reading glasses perched on top of her head. They had only chatted twice now, but already her open bearing and lively manner had drawn Kate to her.

"I'm serious," Kate said. "They started working without being asked. Not many kids will do that without someone giving the order." She smiled at the memories of her own kids. "Or offering some other incentive."

Livvy quirked a brow. "Such as bribery?"

Kate laughed. "My own weapon of choice when it came to getting my kids to do something they didn't want to do— and after I'd tried everything else."

"Tell me about your kids."

"We've got three, two daughters and a son. Andrew, our oldest, lives in Philadelphia, works as a lawyer. He's married and has two kids—the cutest grandchildren you'd ever want to see.

"Rebecca's the baby of the family," Kate continued. "She's in New York City, hoping for her big break on the Broadway stage. Right now she's an understudy.

"And our older daughter, Melissa, lives in Atlanta. She's married and has recently presented us with our third grandchild, a little girl named Mia Elizabeth."

"They sound like great kids."

Kate's eyes filled with tears. Embarrassed, she reached for a nearby tissue box. "The older two have been out of the nest for some time, but Rebecca's wingspreading is still pretty new."

Livvy seemed to see right through to Kate's soul. "Something tells me all this—the move, the new church, new home, the empty nest—is harder on you than you're letting on."

Kate blew her nose and shrugged it off with a laugh. "Sometimes it does seem a bit overwhelming."

"You've got a friend, Kate. It's me. I've just appointed myself, and it's official. If you ever need to talk, I'm your woman. If you ever need anything . . ."—she glanced around the room at the stacks of boxes—"and you do! Beginning this week, I'm coming over to help you unpack."

Kate started to raise her hand in protest, but Livvy shook her head. "As your new friend, I'm telling you that you have no choice in the matter." She leaned forward conspiratorially. "And if you decide to redecorate, I've got a stack of interior decorating magazines three feet high." She laughed. "Of course, with two teenagers of the male variety—our home is decorated in sweat socks and football jerseys. Ahh, but someday . . ." Her gaze lingered on the sliders for an instant. She frowned, then turned back to Kate. "Anyone ever tell you that you've got a herd of sheep on your windows?"

Kate threw back her head and laughed. That cinched it. This was a woman with an artistic eye. "You couldn't have offered anything better. When can we start?"

The men had finished with the chairs, and Danny called to Livvy that they were ready to leave.

Kate walked Livvy to the front door, but Livvy hesitated before stepping outside. "I couldn't help overhearing Renee tell you that she recognized the arsonist from someplace." She paused. "The odd thing about it is that when I saw him during the fire, I had the strangest feeling I knew him from somewhere too."

"Is he from around here?"

Livvy shook her head. "Not that I know of."

"I saw him just for an instant, but I was struck by how utterly sad he looked. It was as if so much sorrow had filled his heart, he couldn't bear to go on."

Danny came up the walk to stand beside his wife. "Are you talking about the arsonist?"

The women nodded.

"I recognized him—maybe from newspaper clippings or photos, something like that. It's likely he's been caught doing something like this before."

"Newspaper clippings . . ." Livvy mused, narrowing her eyes. "That gives me an idea. I'll check the archives tomorrow."

Kate frowned. "Archives?"

Livvy smiled. "Oh, I don't think I told you. I'm the town librarian. Anything and everything you want to know, come to me and I'll find it out for you."

Chapter Five

After nearly thirty years of marriage, Paul still had the ability to make her heart flutter. There were those little things she loved about him, of course—the way he combed his fingers through his hair when he was puzzled about something, the way his eyes brightened when he caught her watching him, or the way he threw back his head and laughed at her jokes, even when she couldn't remember the punch line. She loved how he warmed her cup with hot water before pouring her first cup of coffee. But what she loved most about her husband, when all was said and done, was the way he lived out God's grace, giving to others what his Lord had so freely given him. It was part of who he was. Correction: it was *all* of who he was.

This was one of those times that reminded her of his character.

They were sitting together at the kitchen table over coffee. The local paper was spread out before them with the arsonist's photograph plastered across the front page, the headline reading in two-inch-high letters: DRIFTER CONFESSES TO ARSON.

"What do you think would drive a man to set a church on fire?"

Paul looked up. "My first guess would be anger at God. Probably coming from a place of great pain. He needs our prayers, not our anger. He needs us to show him God's redemptive love, not a vindictive, get-even attitude."

These were similar to the words he had spoken after the service the day before. He leaned forward earnestly. "Perhaps he's mentally ill; there's always that concern. But what if this man just made a mistake? What if the act came from a place of unspeakable pain? What if we gave him the opportunity to turn his life around? Isn't that what God would have us do?"

Kate reached for his hand. "You're talking about grace. But not everyone sees it the way you do."

He gave her one of the lopsided smiles she loved. "And there's the law, of course. If he did indeed start the fire, there will be consequences. Severe, I suspect."

"But that doesn't have to stop this congregation from extending forgiveness and grace to him, just as God extends it to us."

"That's what I love about you," Paul said, standing. "You so readily give what God has given you."

She smiled. "Funny . . . I was just thinking the same thing about you."

Paul bent to kiss her cheek before heading out the door for a breakfast meeting at the Country Diner with Danny Jenner, who was a math teacher at the high school.

Kate gathered the dishes and headed to the counter. As she rinsed them and placed them in the dishwasher, something nipped at the edges of her mind. Something she couldn't quite put her finger on.

She rinsed a juice glass, reached to put it in the rack, then stopped and frowned, puzzling over what she knew so far. A man had confessed to setting the fire. Some townspeople thought they recognized him. But the newspaper account said he was a transient. How could they recognize someone who had just recently drifted into town?

Thinking back to the brief moment her eyes had met his, she had to admit there was something about him that was familiar to her too. Was it simply the pain in his eyes that seemed to reach out to her, or did she, too, know him from someplace or from some news account?

Words from the book of Matthew came to her: "I was hungry, and you didn't feed me. I was thirsty, and you didn't give me anything to drink. I was a stranger, and you didn't invite me into your home. I was naked, and you gave me no clothing. I was sick and in prison, and you didn't visit me."

"Surely you don't mean me, right now, do you, Lord?"

She looked around the kitchen and into the dining room and the living room beyond. There were boxes still waiting to be unpacked, the master-bedroom closet, where the movers had dumped their clothes, was calling her name, and she had planned to hang her cookware today to give herself more counter space. Cooking was her hobby, and preparing a favorite gourmet meal, her first since moving in, would be therapeutic for both her and Paul.

No. She was definitely too busy to stop by the jail and visit the arsonist.

She finished the dishes and headed to the garage for the ladder. For two days she had anticipated hanging her prized Williams-Sonoma pots and pans. First, she would measure

the space, then pick up some sort of hanging pot rack at the
hardware store and make a quick stop by the market to buy
the ingredients for a favorite one-pot meal: lamb stew with
rosemary, garlic, and red potatoes.

Saturday night, LuAnne Matthews, a waitress at the local
diner, had stopped by with fresh-baked lasagna, and Sunday
night, Livvy had sent her boys over with a homemade fried
chicken dinner, complete with mashed potatoes, gravy, and
green beans. There were plenty of leftovers, but Kate couldn't
wait to cook her first meal in her own kitchen.

She was at the top of the ladder, reaching over the
counter with a measuring tape, when the words drifted
into her heart again: *I was sick and in prison, and you didn't
visit me.*

She hesitated, staring at the measuring tape for a
moment, then went back to work.

I was sick and in prison, and you didn't visit me.

This time she put the tape down and descended the ladder. With a sigh, she lifted her eyes heavenward and smiled.
"Okay, Lord. I get it. I'm on my way."

She grabbed her pocketbook and keys and raced out of
the house . . . only to come to a dead stop when she reached
the garage. Paul had taken her car to his meeting because his
Lexus hadn't arrived yet.

She stood by the empty garage for a moment, looking
down the street, trying to remember how far it was to town.
She was still deciding whether to attempt the walk when an
Oldsmobile, pale pink and at least two dozen years old,
cruised up with a rumble and stopped in front of her house.
It was in remarkably good condition, but it reminded Kate of

a giant pink Sub-Zero refrigerator on wheels. The passenger-side window rolled down, and when Kate saw the driver, she swallowed a groan and attempted a friendly smile.

"Good morning, Renee."

The older woman sniffed. "It looks like you're on your way someplace."

"I was. But I'd forgotten that Paul took the car this morning."

"You have only one car?"

Kate ignored the dig. "We hired some students from our old church to drive Paul's. They'll be here next week. I hope."

"Oh. I'll be happy to drive you wherever you were headed."

"No, no. That's not necessary," Kate said quickly.

"But you'll have to sit in back. Kisses thinks the front seat is his."

"Truly. It's all right. I'll wait for Paul."

I was sick and in prison, and you didn't visit me.

Kate drew in a deep breath and gave Renee another smile. "Actually, I do think I'll take you up on your offer. If you could drop me . . ." She hesitated. It hadn't taken more than one conversation with the woman to identify her as a busybody. She really didn't want Renee to know where she was headed. Or why. But neither could she lie. "The . . . ah . . . town hall," she finally said. After all, in a town this size, the town hall served a multitude of functions—offices for the mayor, the sheriff's deputy, a small jail, and a large multipurpose room for community get-togethers. She could be heading there for a myriad of reasons.

"Sure. Hop in."

Kate scooted in and buckled up. The fact that conversation was a bit awkward with Kate in the back didn't stop Renee. As she aimed the big vehicle back into the street, she launched right into where she had stopped during the previous day's service. It was all about the arsonist.

Her head barely topped the upper edge of the steering wheel, which she gripped tightly with both hands. Kisses had moved from his seat to stand on Renee's lap, nose pointing out the open window. Keeping the Oldsmobile pointed toward town, Renee glanced over her shoulder at Kate. "Did you hear that he confessed?"

"It was in this morning's paper."

"I knew he was guilty as dirt. I told you that yesterday."

"He needs our prayers, not our condemnation."

Renee shot her a look. "He needs to pay for what he did."

Kate settled back into the seat and prayed for grace. An abundance of grace. "The courts will sort it out, I'm sure."

Renee rolled her eyes. "Courts? Ha. He'll never get his due, believe you me. I can't abide those soft-touch do-gooders who'll probably find a way to get him off. I tell you what... I'm planning to do a little digging myself. Make sure he doesn't get off with little more than a hand slap."

Kate was getting worried about Renee looking at her instead of at the road. She added traveling mercies to her prayer for grace.

Renee turned back to look at the road just in time to swerve out of the way of a school bus. Kate grabbed the armrest, knuckles white, and breathed a sigh of relief.

"As I was saying, he hurt a lot of people. Most of our congregation can tell you about the special occasions we celebrated at Faith Briar—weddings, funerals, baptisms. Those are moments you can't ever get back, not even in a new church." She shook her head. "Nosiree, that arsonist robbed us of more than just a building; he robbed us of a special place that was ours alone. And believe you me, he's going to pay."

But it wasn't yours—ours—alone, Kate wanted to argue. It was the house of the Lord, and he will restore what was taken from us. But she thought it wise to keep her thoughts to herself.

Renee turned right on Hamilton, left on Euclid, then maneuvered the big car down into a parking space by the town hall. She was surprisingly adept, considering that parking the thing looked about as manageable as docking the *Queen Elizabeth II*. Renee turned around and raised a thin-penciled brow Kate's direction. "What's your business here, then?"

Kate gave her a sweet smile as she slid out of the big car. "Just business," she said. "Thanks for the ride, Renee. I really appreciate it." She closed the door and turned to leave.

"But how will you get home?"

Kate turned and waved. "Don't worry. I'll find Paul—"

"I'll wait for you!" Renee reached for the door handle. "Better yet, I'll come in with you." She was out of the car before Kate could protest.

"Really," she said. "That's not neces—"

"Not an inconvenience at all," Renee said, clipping a jeweled leash on Kisses. The little dog hopped down, sat, and looked up at Kate with large bug eyes. He was shivering even though he sported a hand-crocheted sweater the same shade as the car.

The town hall was a no-nonsense two-story brick building with off-white trim. Maple trees, just beginning to turn, lined the walkway leading to the concrete stairs and the double glass-door entrance. Patches of autumn-dry grass spread out beneath the trees.

Renee huffed and puffed as she followed Kate along the walkway, up the stairs, then through the glass doors.

A uniformed guard stood to one side, holding a clipboard, and watched them approach. Kate spotted the sign for the deputy's office to the right of the entrance and turned to wait for Renee.

The cat would soon be out of the bag—or would have been if the guard hadn't stopped Renee.

"Sorry, ma'am, the dog isn't allowed in here."

Renee stopped dead still, glaring. "First of all," she said, "Kisses is no ordinary dog. He is a purebred toy Chihuahua. I have the papers to prove it. And secondly . . ."—she tapped the deputy's chest with her index finger.

"Sorry, ma'am," the guard said, though his voice had dropped to a kinder timbre, "but you cannot proceed. New regulations. We had an incident with a Saint Bernard a few weeks ago. Since then, no pets."

Renee stared at him, her eyes watering. "Well I never," she finally muttered.

"I'll only be a few minutes," Kate said.

Renee checked her nails, sighed, then led Kisses back down the steps to her car.

A few strides across the creaking wooden floor, and Kate pushed through the door leading to the deputy's office. A uniformed man sat at the front desk.

"I'd like to speak to the man you arrested for arson."

The young man glanced up at her with a frown, and she realized he was the same red-haired sheriff's deputy who had passed them on their way into town. He looked younger than her daughter Rebecca, which meant he was barely into his twenties.

He was still frowning, perhaps in an attempt to appear stern, which he probably thought was befitting his position. But the result was almost comical. The end of his freckled nose took a bit of a tweak to the left, probably from an old football accident, and his dark hazel eyes seemed too ready to smile. Plus, it was hard to take seriously someone with the name Skip, which was printed on his nametag.

He blinked. "You mean Jed Brawley?"

"I wasn't aware he had told anyone his name."

"We don't think he's telling us the truth, and he has no identification. So far we haven't heard back on his prints."

"So, Jed Brawley it is for now."

"Yep." The kid twiddled his pencil in his fingers, then stuck it over his ear. After a moment, he took it down again and tapped the eraser on the table.

"It doesn't matter to me what his name is, I would still like to see him."

"You mean here? Today?"

She sighed. "Yes, here. Right now."

Deputy Skip looked skeptical. "Well, I don't know. I'd have to ask the sheriff. I really can't make a decision of this magnitude . . . I mean, the sheriff works mainly out of Pine Ridge and comes into Copper Mills on his rounds. But then, he *is* just over at the burn site. You could go over there and check, but that's not the usual sort of . . . But then, even the fire wasn't the usual, well, you might say . . ."

Kate held up a hand. "If the sheriff were here, would he allow a visitor in to see Jed Brawley?"

"Well, now. I don't know for sure. Depends on the visitor, I suppose."

Kate leaned over his desk. "Okay, then, let's try this. Has Jed retained an attorney?"

He shook his head.

"I assume he's been allowed his one phone call?" She didn't know for sure that placing a call was a prisoner's right, but she'd seen it on *Matlock* and thought she'd give it a stab.

"Now, that I know for sure. He didn't want to talk to anyone. Not a soul."

"Until me. I think he'll want to see me."

The young man frowned again but didn't ask why, probably because he was raised to be polite. That might not be a good quality in police work.

She smiled at him. "Deputy, I just want to talk with Jed, see if he needs anything, let him know the people of Faith Briar are praying for him."

Two red eyebrows shot heavenward. "You're from the church he burned down?"

She nodded.

He shook his head slowly, his expression full of admiration. "And you came here to talk with him?"

"Yes."

"About praying for him?"

"Well, partially, yes, that's why."

The kid let out a slow whistle. "Well, now, I can't find any fault with that. I don't imagine the sheriff would either. My own grandma and grandpa are members there." He gave her a closer look. "What did you say your name is?"

"Kate Hanlon."

"You must be the new minister's wife. I heard my folks talking about how strange it was that the church burned to the ground on the day the Hanlons arrived." He picked up the phone on his desk, mumbled a few words, then tilted his head toward the double doors across the hall. "Wait there. Someone will be out shortly to take you to see Brawley."

JED BRAWLEY DIDN'T LOOK UP as she approached the second cell in the two-cell jail. He just sat as still as an iron-clad statue on the edge of a metal cot, his head in his hands.

"What do you want?" he mumbled.

"I just wanted to see if you're all right."

With that, he lifted his head and gave her a short, bitter laugh. "All right?" He laughed again. It was a haunting sound.

"Why did you do it?" She could have kicked herself for asking. It hadn't been her intention. But now it was too late. And as Paul liked to say, you can't un-ring a bell.

Jed didn't seem to mind the question. He shrugged and dropped his head again. "Sometimes fire attracts those who deserve God's wrath. I am one of those."

"But why?" She stepped closer. "Why Faith Briar Church?"

He looked up, frowning. "The flames, the heat, the rush of knowing that punishment follows for the wicked."

She took another step closer to the iron-barred barrier between them. "Did something happen at the church to make you so bitter? Is that why you felt you needed to punish . . ." She hesitated. She was treading on dangerous ground, entering the territory someone better trained in psychology should handle. But something drove her to complete the thought. ". . . to punish God?"

He stared at her without blinking and then laughed. A soft, eerie laugh that rocked his shoulders. "Punish God? Oh no. It's me who's in need of punishment, don't you see? The flames, the heat, the punishment of the wicked that follows —it all lands on my shoulders, for I am the wicked one." His words were stilted, as if he had said them to himself so many times, they were memorized.

She could ask again why he did it, but it seemed they were already playing round-robin. He had confessed to the crime, and that was that. She would leave the rest to the experts. She went back to the real reason for her visit.

"I'm sorry I questioned you," she said. "That really wasn't my intent. I actually came to see if you need anything. Can I contact your relatives, friends, or anyone to let them know where you are?"

The haunted look in his eyes returned. "There is no one," he said. "No one at all."

"Has anyone spoken to you about legal counsel?"

His mouth twisted into a sneer. "Haven't you been listening? I felt the heat of the flames, and in them I saw the faces of death. I've confessed to the crime. I need no counsel. I'm guilty as charged." He moved closer, his presence menacing. "You're not needed or wanted. Now get out."

Kate blinked in surprise at the sudden aggression. "I'll be back," she said softly. "And I want you to know I'm praying for you."

He stared at her, his face ragged and weary. "Don't," he said, this time his voice was void of bitterness. "I'm not worth your time or effort." He turned his back on her.

She headed back to the door at the end of the corridor, already planning her next step: a visit to the site where the church once stood. Something about Jed's confession bothered her, and she wanted to find out what it was. Taking a look at the evidence proving the fire was arson was a logical place to start.

RENEE'S PINK VEHICLE was still parked in the lot beside the town hall, but she was a short distance away letting Kisses raise his leg on a patch of grass. "Ahh, there you are," she said as Kate approached.

"I don't want to keep you any longer from whatever you have planned for the day," she said to Renee. "I've got other errands to run, then I'll catch Paul at the Country Diner. He can drive me home."

"No reason I can't go with you," Renee said, heading to the car. "The only appointments I have today are a manicure and pedicure at noon and a facial at three."

Kate gave her a tight smile. "No, really, I'm fine. Honestly, I don't want to take up any more of your time."

Renee's eyes looked made of steel, and there was a determined set to her jaw. She brushed an errant bleached-blond strand of hair away from her face. "Then at least let me take you by the diner to make sure the pastor is there. I would feel terrible to know you didn't have a way home."

The woman was tenacious. And caring, Kate had to admit. She sighed. "All right, then. The diner it is." She would wait until she had the car to visit the site of the burned church. Kate settled into the backseat of the Oldsmobile and fastened her seat belt.

Renee looked at her through the rearview mirror. "I bet the sheriff is nosing around the church. If he's up to snuff, he oughtta be. How about if we take a little detour on our way to the diner and have a look-see?"

Kate stifled a groan. "*Hmm*. That would be interesting," she said.

"You bet," Renee said happily as she backed the Sub-Zero out of the parking slot. "It'll be the first step in my personal investigation."

THE SITE MOVED KATE to tears. Even Renee seemed speechless. There, spread out before them, lay a heap of ashes. The stench of wet debris filled their nostrils. Renee let go of the steering wheel with one hand, waved her fingers in front of her nose, then dove into her designer pocketbook for a handkerchief.

Off to one side, the sheriff was stooped over, fingering through what looked like a handful of ashes. He stood in what might have been part of the sanctuary, with a partially crumbling brick wall on one side, the blackened hull of the church bell on the other, and the soggy, charred remnants of the once-proud steeple lying in repose behind him.

Kate sniffed, her heart aching for the people of Faith Briar. Renee aimed the big car to the side of the road, slowed, and set the emergency brake. Before Kate could unlatch her seat belt, the older woman had gathered Kisses in her arms and leaped from the car.

By the time Kate exited, Renee was marching, chin jutting, toward the sheriff. When he looked up, his expression
was glum, and Kate guessed it wasn't just because of the task
he was performing. His icy stare and clenched jaw said Renee
Lambert was the last person in the world he wanted to see.

"Sheriff Roberts! What luck that you're here!"

Kate could almost hear him groan. She knew the feeling.

"Renee," he said with a nod, his voice businesslike.

"What have you found? Anything to link the perp to the
crime? Keep him in the slammer."

"Perp?"

She nodded. "That's what I said, the perp."

He glanced at Kate as Renee approached. For a split second, it seemed his quick cough covered a laugh. "Perp," he
finally said. "*Hunh*." Then he turned back to the sample of
soil and soot he was sifting.

"Well?" Renee said.

Sheriff Roberts didn't answer.

"We should be going," Kate said to Renee. "Let's leave the
sheriff to his work."

Renee ignored her. "I leave you with one word," she said,
stepping closer to the sheriff, "and it's one I expect you not to
forget."

He looked up with a sigh. "What's that, Renee?"

"Justice."

He stood, brushing off his hands and frowning. "What?"

"You heard me. Justice! We can't let this perp beat this
rap." With that pronouncement, she spun and, chin once
again jutting, marched back to the car.

Sheriff Roberts caught Kate's eye and, shoulders shaking

with silent laughter, reached for his handkerchief and blew his nose with gusto. "You ever hear about the time my deputy arrested Renee Lambert for petty theft?"

Kate shook her head.

"It seems she was adjusting Joe Tucker's handkerchief, and Skip thought she was trying to pick the old man's pocket. Happened last summer at the Fourth of July parade. I'd told him to be on the lookout for pickpockets, and he got a tad overzealous." This time the sheriff chuckled out loud. "The kid has the right intentions, but he's a thorn in my side at times. I keep having to bump him back to a desk job. Then there's poor Renee. She never got over it."

He gave Kate a closer look. "You're the new pastor's wife, aren't you?"

She stuck out her hand. "I'm afraid we haven't been introduced properly, but yes, I am. My name's Kate Hanlon."

"Nice to meet you, Miz Hanlon. I'm sorry for what happened to your church. But I think we got our perp, as Renee calls him. He confessed to the crime, and all the evidence points that direction."

"It looks like you're still investigating."

"Most of the evidence adds up, but some doesn't. Skip said he spotted evidence of arson the day of the fire, but I'm not finding it."

Kate knelt to pick up a handful of muddy ashes. She carefully rubbed the clump between her thumb and fingers. On closer examination, she could see tiny shards of red glass mixed with the gray black mud. "This must have been near the altar."

Sheriff Roberts knelt beside her. "What did you find?"

"Remnants of candles. The holders, not the candles, obviously."

"Near as I can tell, the fire seemed to have started here— at least it was the early source of the flames."

"What doesn't add up?"

He gave her a sharp look, and she knew she'd asked a question he wouldn't—or couldn't—answer. "We're still investigating," he said.

"You said the source of the fire was here by the altar."

He nodded.

"Interesting," she said, narrowing her eyes in thought. "If someone were trying to set a church on fire, wouldn't there be more than one source? I would think it would be easier to get away if the fire was set on the outside."

He studied her for a moment. "Not necessarily. Too easily spotted. If it's a raging fire you want, you set it inside, then run. Then nobody knows until it's too late." The sheriff turned back to sifting ashes. "Whatever Skip said he found is now covered by a ton of mud," he muttered, shaking his head. "I told him to take a photograph, but did he listen? Nosiree. Now I've gotta just keep digging."

Behind them Renee tooted the horn in the pink Oldsmobile. Kate thanked the sheriff for his time and hurried toward the vehicle.

A few minutes later, Renee aimed the car into a U-turn and stopped in front of the library, another two-story brick building, though it was somewhat smaller than the town hall. They looked to have been built around the same time, and possibly designed by the same architect. The only difference was dark green trim instead of ivory.

"I'll wait in case you need a ride," she said with a look on her face that said there would be no arguing.

LIVVY JENNER WAS STANDING behind a large horseshoe-shaped counter at the library entrance. She looked up with a smile as Kate approached. Behind the counter was a door with Livvy's name on it and the title "head librarian" underneath her name.

A few people were reading at nearby tables, and Kate could see a teenager replacing books in the stacks to the right of the counter.

They exchanged greetings, then Kate asked if Livvy had found out anything about the arsonist.

Livvy nodded. "I think I've got a lead, some puzzling stuff." She glanced at the clock behind the desk. "I can't get away today, but how about if we meet for lunch at the diner tomorrow? I should know more by then and can tell you what I've found out."

Outside, Renee honked the car horn, and inside, Kate sighed. Livvy gave her an understanding smile. "Tomorrow, then," Kate said with a wave and a chuckle as she headed to the door.

"I'VE DECIDED WHERE THE BELL needs to go," Renee said once Kate had fastened her seat belt.

"Where?"

"It just came to me. It needs to be where everyone can see it on a regular basis. It will keep our hopes up through this crisis."

"That's a good idea." Kate considered places in town that could house a bell that big. Nothing came to her. "Where?" she asked again.

Renee aimed the vehicle onto the road and, still moving forward, looked over her shoulder at Kate. "Your backyard."

"My backyard?"

"Where else?"

"I don't know how something that big and heav—"

Renee swerved to miss an oncoming car. "That's the easy part. But we'll need to find a crane."

"Our house?" Kate said again. "You're sure?"

But Renee had turned back around and was happily humming a Christmas song about bells.

Chapter Six

Kate met Livvy outside the diner the next day at noon. As soon as they stepped inside, they were greeted by the scent of apple pies baking, coffee brewing, and hamburgers sizzling. Nearly all the tables and booths were filled, but Kate followed Livvy to an empty spot in the corner by a blue-gingham-curtained window.

People called out greetings, and Livvy took Kate by a few tables to make introductions. Then she stopped at the booth next to where they were about to be seated.

Three men looked up and smiled. One wore a clerical collar.

"Let me introduce Pete MacKenzie, pastor of Copper Mill Presbyterian; Bobby Evans, pastor of the First Baptist, and Lucas Gregory, rector at St. Lucy's Episcopal." The latter was the one with the collar.

"Some refer to this table as the holy of holies," Bobby laughed. "Tell your husband he's got an open invitation to join us. We try to meet weekly but can't always get away from our flocks. We can promise him, though, that when we do meet, we have some pretty lively discussions."

"But all in brotherly love," Father Lucas said.

Pastor Pete grinned. "Maybe your husband can straighten out these two on their stubborn theological views."

The others laughed. "You wish."

As soon as Kate and Livvy were seated, LuAnne Matthews bustled over with two empty mugs and a pot of coffee. "Leaded or unleaded?" She was dressed in a polyester dress with a no-nonsense white apron. She looked like she'd stepped right out of the 1950s, even down to the jeweled-eyeglass chain that draped around her neck. She had a ready laugh, short red hair that looked like it came out of a bottle, and a round face with a smattering of freckles.

Kate laughed. "Looks like you brought the right pot. Leaded, please."

"How you holdin' up, darlin'?" she asked as she poured coffee in both cups.

"We've barely begun unpacking, if that's what you mean."

LuAnne smiled. "No, actually I meant about landin' here in the middle of nowhere with the church you came to serve burned to the ground." She glanced heavenward and sighed. "This town needs all the heavenly help it can get. And the two of you do too," she said. "And I'm not just talkin' about taking your dishes outta boxes and lining your shelves with contact paper. It can't be easy pullin' up roots and starting over . . . then to have something like this happen . . ." She tsk-tsked as she headed to the cash register, where two customers were waiting to pay their bill.

"Now," Livvy said, leaning closer. "About the arsonist . . . I've been wracking my brain, trying to make a connection, but it's eluding me. I may be putting two and two together and coming up with three . . ."

"What do you have?"

"As I said, there may not be any connection, but I found two photos of a man named J. B. Packer who was a star athlete and valedictorian of his senior class at Copper Mill High. The guy was good looking and popular, featured in the local paper during the three years he played varsity football, then again when he was elected student body president his senior year. He was also crowned homecoming king that same fall."

"And you think he's connected to Jed Brawley?"

"I admit it's a stretch. But so many people thought they'd seen Brawley before, I tried the *Chronicle* archives. It didn't go anywhere, so I went to the school newspaper archives. They don't have many back issues converted to electronic files yet, so again, I ended up with nothing."

She leaned across the table. "Then I remembered my kids talking about the popularity of Web sites like schoolmates.com where former classmates find one another and announce homecomings, reunions, that sort of thing. This particular site posts photographs from yearbooks going back to the dark ages. I thought I just might recognize him." She shrugged. "Again, nothing turned up."

She paused for a sip of coffee. "Next I scanned the messages posted from former students through the years. Because it's a small school, there weren't too many. The heading, 'Where are they now?' caught my attention. Some girl who had a crush on J.B. in high school was trying to find him. She went on and on about this good-looking kid, his accomplishments, also about the fact that he married his high-school sweetheart and left town the summer after graduation and was never heard from again.

"I then did a search for the initials, J.B., and that's when the *Chronicle* archives pulled up the information. The kid looks pretty ragged and worn in those game shots. And I still don't know if he could be Jed Brawley. It's a shot in the dark."

She reached into her handbag and pulled out two pieces of paper. She unfolded each and laid them side by side on the table between them. "See what you think."

Two grainy black-and-white photographs stared up at Kate. The one on the left was of a young couple, obviously the newly crowned homecoming king and queen. They were looking at each other instead of at the camera. Even in the grainy, rough photo, it was clear they were in love.

"This is J.B.'s high-school sweetheart, the one he married after graduation. According to the caption, her maiden name was Rachelle Kensington."

Kate picked up the second photo and brought it closer. It was of a high-school kid in a football uniform, sweaty and covered with mud and grass stains. With his helmet on and blackened cheekbones, he could have been anyone. "I agree," she said. "It's a bit of a stretch." She started to hand the photo back to Livvy, then stopped. "Wait, there *is* something—"

"Well, ladies," LuAnne Matthews said at her elbow. "What'd you decide on? Pie à la mode, tuna melt on rye— now that's a sandwich to die for—or maybe our specialty of the day, a half rack of baby backs with slaw and barbecue beans on the side ... ?"

She stood by the table, grinning down at them. Then her expression changed. Her gaze was fixed on one of the photos. "Well, if that don't beat all," she said. "Mind if I have a closer look?"

Before either Kate or Livvy could answer, she snatched up both pictures and held them to the light. "Well, I'll be," she said again, then dropped into the booth with the women.

LuAnne adjusted her eyeglasses, still staring at the photographs. "I haven't thought of him in years. Why are you two starin' at his photograph like it was the key to some long-lost secret?"

"Because it is," Kate and Livvy said in unison, then laughed.

"Does he look like anyone you've seen lately?" Kate asked, studying LuAnne's face for a flicker of recognition.

She shook her head. "I heard he moved away years ago. Him and that cute little gal of his." She held the picture closer. "J. B. Packer. That does beat all, but no, he doesn't look like anyone I've seen lately."

"What about Jed Brawley?" Kate said. "Do you see a resemblance?"

"Brawley?" LuAnne let out a snort of a laugh. "Brawley's not even in the same league with this kid." She paused. "Of course, this J.B. business was years ago. But even given the wearin' down of a body over time, he couldn't have changed this much."

Livvy sighed. "Well, I guess that's our answer."

"You two thinkin' this is the same man?" She leaned in closer.

"I thought maybe he was," Livvy said.

Kate settled back and crossed her arms. "Take another look. I think Livvy is onto something."

They both frowned and grabbed a photograph as she continued.

"Look at this kid's teeth. Do you see what I see? He's got a small gap between his two front teeth, slight but noticeable." Kate squinted. "And there on his left side—you can see it in both pictures—he's got a chip in his tooth. Tiny, but significant enough to be noticeable."

"I never noticed it," LuAnne said. "Or the gap."

"I did," Kate said. "When I met with him."

"You went to see the arsonist?" LuAnne said, admiration in her eyes. "I'm impressed. You've got guts, and smarts too."

"And a caring heart," Livvy added.

"So you really think they're the same person?" LuAnne asked, squinting at the photograph again. "The arsonist and Jed Brawley?"

"I'm sure of it," Kate said, nodding.

Loretta Sweet, the Country Diner's owner and cook, popped her head out of the service window, and LuAnne hurriedly slid out of the booth.

"Darlin's, here I sit chewin' the fat when I haven't even taken your order. What'll it be?"

They decided to split the tuna melt, and LuAnne scribbled their orders on a well-worn pad, then turned to leave.

She'd only taken a few steps when she turned back. "Speakin' of the arsonist, I overheard something interesting earlier this mornin'."

She stepped back to their table and leaned low, speaking in a conspiratorial whisper. "There were a couple of city slickers in for breakfast. They were talkin' about the big plans they've got for Copper Mill." She leaned in closer. "I only heard bits and snatches, but it sounded like they're in town to finalize some sort of a deal for buyin' land over by the creek. Said something about a fancy spa resort and were talkin' about coming back with some investors."

Livvy frowned. "You think that has something to do with the church fire?" She looked thoughtful. "Danny did say something about a corporation approaching the church board about buying the property. The name was Worldwide Destination Resorts."

"That's the one," LuAnne said. "I'm sure I heard one of them refer to it." She shrugged as she straightened up. "What if they're in cahoots with the arsonist? Maybe they wanted the property so bad, they hired him to do their dirty work."

Kate mulled it over for a few seconds. "There's still something that bothers me about this." She frowned. "We're assuming Jed Brawley, or J. B. Packer, if that's his real name, is guilty."

"He confessed," LuAnne reminded her.

"Lots of people confess to crimes they didn't commit. You hear about that after major forest fires all the time." She shrugged. "I don't know why, but it happens. What if he didn't do it?"

"So, you're sayin', then, that . . ." Behind LuAnne, customers were calling for fresh coffee or water refills. She called out "Just a minute," without turning.

Kate saw Pastor Pete step behind the counter, pick up the coffeepot, and start making the rounds from table to table.

"Thanks, Pete," LuAnne hollered, then turned back to Kate and Livvy. "If that's the case, the corporation might have tapped somebody else to do their dirty work." She paused. "And that would be a whole 'nother kettle of fish."

Livvy and Kate nodded.

"Either way, I'll keep my eyes peeled," LuAnne said. "If those characters from that resort outfit come back"—she winked—"I'll make sure their coffee doesn't have a chance to get cold, so to speak. I can hover, ears wide open, with the best of them."

BY THE TIME KATE ARRIVED HOME, Paul was there with the telephone technician, and by late afternoon, they were connected to the world again. The word spread fast, and before Paul finished programming their answering machine, they received three calls.

The first was from Renee Lambert, who wanted to know if Kate had talked to Paul about putting the church bell in their backyard.

"Yes, and he agrees that it's a fine plan." Kate glanced through the sheep-spotted sliders and imagined the large cast-metal bell sitting in the middle of the tiny yard. She had to smile. It didn't quite fit in her plans for garden landscaping, but the congregation would love looking out at it on Sunday mornings. "We do need to make sure we have a reputable crane operator."

"I already thought of that," Renee said with a sniff. "Our neighbor in San Antonio had a hot tub dropped through his garage roof when the crane operator released the chains too soon."

Paul looked up and grinned. They had already talked about the same thing happening in their living room with the bell. The decor was bad enough. A bell crashing through the ceiling wouldn't help.

"*Hmmph*," Renee said, then changed the subject. "I'm wondering if I can ask you a favor."

Kate cringed, then immediately felt terrible for her lack of charity. "Of course, Renee. What is it?"

"I need to be gone all day Thursday. It's an appointment I must keep."

Probably an all-day spa treatment, Kate thought, picturing seaweed wraps and hot-stone massages.

"And Kisses can't go with me."

"They don't allow pets?"

Renee ignored the question. "He's used to staying by himself for an hour or so at a time, but I've never left him alone all day."

"Would you like for me to stop by to check on him?"

"Oh no. That would mean you'd need to drive over on the hour. He needs full-time attention. It's much easier if I drop him by in the morning on my way to my appointment."

Across the kitchen, Paul had obviously picked up the thread of conversation and was grinning at Kate.

She couldn't say no, but neither could she imagine a two-pound Chihuahua following her around while she unpacked. What if she stepped on the tiny thing? "Yes, of course, Renee. I'd be happy to."

"I'll bring the ingredients for his meals."

"He doesn't eat regular dog food?"

Paul looked ready to bend double with laughter, and Kate made a face at him.

"Oh goodness, no. I sauté ground meat with a teensy bit of fresh garlic and onions three times a day and serve it warm."

"Serve it warm?" Kate's voice came out in a squeak. She didn't even do anything like that for her kids.

"Kisses loves it that way. You'll see," Renee said happily. "There's one other thing. He has an overactive bladder, and you'll need to make sure you get him out the door at the first sign of need."

Great! Kate thought as Renee said good-bye.

The second call was from Danny Jenner, asking if Paul could use a ride to the diner for the church board meeting when he dropped off Livvy to help Kate the following evening. Most meetings these days were held at the Hanlon home—it seemed like there was some church function every night of the week—but they decided to give Kate a break and let her have the run of her house for the evening.

The third call was from LuAnne Matthews at the diner. "I've been thinkin' about something," she said, "and it's too important to put off. I know Livvy's planning to stop by to help with the unpacking. Could you two use some help? We can chat while we work."

"Of course," Kate said. "I'd like nothing better."

"Be prepared, darlin'," LuAnne said. "What I've got to talk to you about is gonna knock your socks off."

Chapter Seven

K ate gave Paul a quick kiss good-bye as he headed out the door to meet Danny at his SUV. Kate stood in the doorway, waiting for Livvy, and LuAnne drove up a few minutes later. She brought three orders of fried chicken, sweet-potato fries, fried okra, and a side of popcorn shrimp left over from the daily special. Kate put out paper plates, stacked extra napkins in the middle of the table, and the three sat down.

Kate said grace, then they dove in.

"Tell us what you've been mulling over," Kate said to LuAnne.

"I've been thinkin' about the heartache we all feel because of the fire. My parents were married in that church," LuAnne said, her eyes glistening with tears. "My grandfather was one of the original builders, and seeing it turned into a pile of rubble, well, it's causing an ache that's like somebody we loved upped and died."

"You're not alone in how you feel." Livvy reached for LuAnne's hand. "We will rebuild. And soon, I hope."

"But you see, we've got to get the ball rollin'. The sooner we do, the better we'll feel about that empty space where our church used to be. And I've got a plan." She blew her nose. "I've already run it by Betty Anderson, who was in for coffee this afternoon, and Abby Pippins, who's ready to roll with it. Phoebe West stopped by to show me her new baby—the cutest little thing; her name's Violet—and she loved the idea too. And Ellie MacKenzie, Pastor Pete's wife, said she was sure the other ministers' wives would join us. Can you imagine, the Presbyterians, the Baptists, and the Episcopalians all joinin' together to rebuild our church?"

She sat back with a satisfied smile. "Nearly everybody I talked to is ready to roll up their sleeves and jump in." She paused. "Well, with one exception. Renee Lambert thinks it's a terrible idea." She blew her nose again, then said under her breath, "Probably because she didn't think of it."

Kate started to say, "But it's only been a few days since the fire," or "Shouldn't we wait to hear what the church board decides?" or "Maybe we ought to wait for the insurance settlement?" but looking at LuAnne's expectant face, she thought better of it. She was beginning to realize the women of Copper Mill were a strong sort and obviously not used to sitting around waiting for the church board or the menfolk to take the lead.

In San Antonio, meetings and focus groups and reports from experts in any given field preceded every plan of action. Sometimes it seemed that meetings were held just to plan the next meeting. Getting any new project off the ground was agonizingly slow.

Not here, she was finding out. Not much got in the way of the ladies of Copper Mill.

Livvy laughed and held up her hands. "Okay, enough fan-fare! We want to know what your plan is."

"Got something to write with?" LuAnne asked Kate. "We need to get down to brass tacks with our plannin'."

Kate cleared the table, tossed the paper plates in the trash, then returned with scratch paper and pens.

"Okay, here's the deal," LuAnne said. "We'll put on a pumpkin festival."

"A pumpkin festival?" Kate hoped her voice didn't reflect her disappointment. She pictured a pumpkin-raising contest and couldn't imagine how the proceeds might help build the new church.

"It's late in the season to plan anything like this," Livvy said gently. "Maybe next year . . ."

"Listen a minute before you dismiss the idea. Have you two heard of the pumpkin festival that Circleville, Ohio, puts on? It's world famous."

Both women shook their heads.

"How does bringing in a cool hundred thou or so sound to you?"

"You're kidding," breathed Livvy. "A hundred thousand dollars?"

LuAnne sat back with a satisfied smile. "Of course, Circleville's been puttin' on their festival for a hundred years. We can't expect our proceeds to quite match theirs. But what if we could even bring in ten thousand, maybe enough to pay for hangin' the church bell again. Maybe even pay for rebuild-ing the steeple?" Her eyes filled, and she dabbed at them with her tissue. "Don't you see? If we get busy working, just doing something, anything, to feel like we're taking some steps forward, it would do wonders for our spirits."

Livvy smiled. "We can do it," she said. "I know we can."

Kate had already started making notes. "An arts-and-crafts fair," she murmured, writing it down. "We'll get the ladies of the church to get started with their knitting, crocheting, weaving, quilting. There will be an entry fee, we'll give out ribbons, then sell the items later."

"A best pumpkin-pie contest," Livvy said, scribbling on her pad. "Entry fees there too. Then the pies will be for sale."

"Pumpkin contest," LuAnne said, and wrote it down. "A prize for the largest, the ugliest, and the cutest."

"Isn't it too late in the season to grow them?" Kate asked.

"Most folks around here are already growin' them. They put them in right after the last of the sunflowers in the summer. We'll just tell them the contest is comin' up, so they can throw on extra fertilizer."

"And we'll crown a Little Miss Pumpkin Princess!" Livvy laughed. "Open to the little ones. Based on best pumpkin costume. Can't you just see it all now?"

"And a Little Mister Pumpkin Prince!" LuAnne added.

They all scribbled furiously, the ideas flying faster than they could write.

"We'll bake the world's largest pumpkin pie!" LuAnne almost shouted, then wrote it down. "We'll call the Guinness Book of World Records." She grinned. "As big as a VW! Or a Mack truck!"

Livvy blinked. "How would you go about baking something that size?"

LuAnne laughed. "You're right. Maybe that's not such a good idea."

"We can make pumpkin grits," Kate said. "With Gorgonzola and sage. I saw a recipe in one of my gourmet magazines. I can find it again—I know I can!"

The other two women looked at her as if she had just stepped off a spaceship from Mars. "Pumpkin grits?" they said in unison.

"Well, yes. I've never tried it, but I can . . ."

"Darlin', this here's the South," LuAnne said, patting her hand. "Now, maybe if you wanted to deep fry 'em in little balls and roll each little ball in cornflakes, folks might take to it. But if they knew those grits had pumpkin in 'em . . ." She shrugged, "well, honestly, I don't think they would sell."

Livvy laughed. "I think we're selling our Copper Mill folk short. If they knew the grits were for a good cause, I bet they'd buy them."

"Then let's serve two kinds—one with pumpkin, one without," Kate said.

"And one spooned out in little balls, deep-fried, and rolled in cornflakes," LuAnne said as she wrote it down. "I'll be in charge of those."

THAT NIGHT PAUL AND KATE sat together in front of the fireplace over tea. Kate had her robe and slippers on and was curled up in the rocker. Paul was sitting next to her, unusually solemn as he stared into the fire.

She reached for his hand. "I take it the board meeting didn't go well."

He sighed deeply. "Actually, the meeting itself went well.

We've got some good people in this church." He gave her a quick smile. "Most of the agenda had to do with pretty heavy issues. But we did have one lighter moment—at least it was for me. It seems there have been complaints about Renee Lambert bringing her little dog to services, so she came fully prepared to get an official approval from me as pastor and Danny as chairman of the board, and even a vote of confidence from the rest of the board members." He chuckled. "She gave a little sermon about Noah's ark and seeing-eye dogs, with a bit of lore thrown in about dogs rescuing their owners. When she was through, she had convinced the board that the little Chihuahua could stay."

His voice softened. "I had to agree. The ark was a sanctuary, a place God ordained to keep his beloved creation safe. Maybe it's not such a bad thing for Renee to bring her dog into ours."

The fire crackled and popped, and Paul sighed again.

"And about those items on the agenda that weren't so light?"

He turned to her, and she could see the concern in his eyes. "Danny stopped by the bank this afternoon after work. He dug through the church's safe-deposit files, hunting for a copy of the insurance policy."

"Thank goodness it wasn't in the church office," Kate said.

Paul frowned. "We all said the same thing until we saw the policy."

Her heart caught. "Something's wrong with it?"

"It seems that it's been years since the policy was updated. It was first taken out twenty-five years ago. The coverage would have been more than adequate back then, but building costs have multiplied astronomically. The church secretary, Millie, had been diligent about paying the premiums right on time, but it seems no one thought about increasing the coverage taking into account rebuilding costs in today's market."

Kate got up and knelt beside his chair, draping her arm around his shoulders. "Oh, Paul . . ."

He took her hand and squeezed her fingers. "First the fire, now this. Can you imagine what this will do to Faith Briar's ability to rebuild? When our parishioners find out, they'll be devastated."

"Does anyone know how much the policy will cover?"

"We haven't met with any construction people yet, but I'm guessing we may have only enough to clear the property to get it ready for rebuilding."

She stood to pour more tea, and when she came back from the kitchen, she sat down on the edge of the rocker, facing Paul.

"One thing I've noticed in the few days we've been here is the incredible resilience and energy of the Faith Briar congregation. They're mourning, yes. But there's also this desire to put the sniffles aside, roll up their sleeves, and get busy with whatever needs doing."

Paul took a sip of tea. "I agree, but what does that have to do with the insurance policy?"

"Did you notice we didn't get any unpacking done tonight?"

His gaze took in the stacked boxes all around them.

"Actually, I didn't." He chuckled. "I guess maybe I'm getting used to these boxes."

"Paul, the ladies have come up with the most amazing plan to raise money for the church." She told him briefly about the pumpkin festival.

He asked a few questions, but she could see his heart wasn't in it. Worry lines were still carved deep into his face.

"You don't think it will work, do you?"

"Honey, I know their hearts—and yours—are in the right place. But we're talking about a huge amount of money. I don't think any single event, a festival or anything else, can make a dent in what we need to get a building program off the ground."

She laughed. "Just you wait, mister. When you get a group of praying women together, just about anything can happen."

Grinning, he held up his hands in surrender. "Okay, okay. I believe you. Just don't sign me up to make pumpkin grits."

"I already did."

Chapter Eight

Renee Lambert rang the doorbell at 7:14 AM. She was dressed in still another set of velveteen workout clothes, this time a dark pink. She carried a small gold lamé handbag with matching tennis shoes and umbrella. Kisses sat shivering on the porch by her ankle, looking up at Kate, his eyes wide. As usual, the Chihuahua was tethered to Renee with a jeweled leash, bedecked in a fuzzy sweater the same shade as Renee's workout clothes.

"Oh dear, Kisses looks cold," Kate said. "Please come in so he can warm up."

Renee bustled past Kate, took in with obvious distaste the still towering stacks of boxes in foyer and living room, then reluctantly stooped to release the clasp on the Chihuahua's collar. "There, there, little snuggle-umpkins," she cooed. "Mommy will be back before you know it."

Kate avoided exchanging a glance with Paul who'd left his coffee at the kitchen table to join them in the foyer.

Renee straightened and nodded to Paul. "Pastor, would you mind getting my little umpkin's food bag out of the car?"

It was an order, not a question. "And don't forget his little bed. It's on the seat in the back."

Paul smiled, took Renee's keys, and headed down the front walk. The man deserved another jewel in his crown.

Renee fished around in her handbag for a sheet of paper with instructions for feeding, nap time, and how to give Kisses a tiny drop of Dramamine from a medicine dropper should "little umpkins" become "upset because of the environment."

Kate received the information with good humor and let out a huge sigh of relief when Renee headed back down the walk to the pink Sub-Zero. Luckily, Kisses immediately curled up in his shearling sheepskin bed, which Paul had placed near the fireplace, and went to sleep. Soon after, the teacup-sized dog let out a snore that could wake neighbors three doors away.

"Don't tell me that's little umpkins," Paul said when she rejoined him in the kitchen.

"This dog weighs less than two pounds—how could he make such a big noise?"

"Adenoids?"

Kate laughed. "Don't tell Renee. She already worries herself sick over this little dog. We don't want to further alarm her."

Paul went back to his morning paper, which was spread over the kitchen table. "Look at this," he said and pushed the front section toward her.

Kate dropped into a chair and read the headline aloud: ARSONIST REMAINS A MYSTERY MAN. His mug shot stared out at the world, a mix of defeat, anger, and sorrow in his eyes.

She scanned the article, which reported nothing new. Law enforcement officials and reporters were obviously still scratching their heads, trying to figure out the arsonist's identity.

"Maybe you should call the sheriff and tell him what you know," Paul suggested.

"I thought about it, but I didn't want to come across as a busybody. I just figured the professionals would come up with the same information we did in half the time."

Paul handed her the phone. "You underestimate yourself, Katie. I'm sure the sheriff will welcome the lead."

She grinned. "How sure?" She imagined how the sheriff's face would look when he found out the pastor's wife and the librarian had figured out the arsonist's ID before anyone in law enforcement.

Paul obviously read her mind. "You've got a point, but you've still got to tell him. He'll appreciate it in the long run."

She punched in the number for the sheriff's office.

The call was picked up on the first ring. Kate recognized Skip's deep voice.

"Is the sheriff in this morning?" she asked.

"He's at his office in Pine Ridge today. I can call over there and ask him to give you a ring."

"Yes, please. It's important. I've got a lead on the arsonist's identity."

"Whoa, you do? Do you . . . ah . . . want to give me the information? I can pass it along."

"Just have him call."

She gave Skip her name and number and then placed the receiver back in its cradle.

Thirty seconds later, the phone rang.

"Hello?"

"This is the sheriff. How can I help you?"

"Thank you for calling. My friend Livvy Jenner, the librarian, and I discovered something we thought you might want to know about."

"And what's that?" He sounded bored, and she pictured him doodling on a notepad.

She explained about the photographs and the connection between J. B. Packer and Jed Brawley.

For a moment he didn't speak. "*Hmm,*" he finally said. "I'll check into it." Then he sighed. Another moment of silence followed. "And I . . . ah . . . want to say thank you, Miz Hanlon . . . for calling that is."

She hung up and grinned at Paul. "I don't think he's used to thanking women for helping out on a case."

Paul chuckled. "He's probably kicking himself around his desk for not coming up with the information first."

They both sobered as they looked back down at the mug shot and article about the arsonist's confession.

"Something's bothering you about this, isn't it?" Paul asked.

"I can't explain why, but I just don't think he set that fire." She thought about it for a minute, then another angle came to her. "Or what if—just what if—he was forced to do it?"

Paul narrowed his eyes in thought. "What do you mean?"

She quickly filled him in on the conversation LuAnne had overheard at the diner.

"Did you know about the group—Worldwide Destination Resorts—that wanted to buy the church property?"

He nodded. "It was brought up at the meeting. Sam

Gorman said maybe we should contact them to see if they're still interested. We'd take the money and buy a smaller piece of land someplace else . . . He said maybe we should talk to Eli Weston about the costs of building a smaller church, how feasible it would be to go this direction. Apparently Eli has some experience as a building contractor."

"But what if this company is behind the fire? I would hate to see us get involved with it until we know it's in the clear." She paused, then added, "Though I can't imagine why anybody would want a piece of property so badly they would resort to such a crime, especially against a church."

"In a word, greed, Katie. Greed." He studied her face for a moment. "You're saying that maybe they coerced Brawley— or Packer—into starting the fire for them?"

"I still don't think he could have done it unless the threat was so great—"

"You mean something like blackmail?"

She tapped the eraser end of a pencil against the newspaper.

"That's a pretty heavy accusation."

"I'm just playing the what-if game."

Paul suddenly smiled. "I know you well. You're dying to go see Packer again and get to the bottom of this, aren't you?"

She grinned.

"And you're about to ask me to babysit umpkins?"

"Would you mind terribly?"

He glanced out at the gray drizzle. "Do you realize I'll be holding an umbrella over this mouse-sized dog with his pink sweater and jeweled leash when he's gotta go? Do you know what that will do to my masculinity?"

She laughed. "You can always take him out to the back-yard. No one will see you."

"*Au contraire*. If I'm going to care for this little critter, I'll take him to the best tree in the neighborhood. And that's the small maple by the front walk."

AN HOUR AND A HALF LATER, fresh baked cookies in hand, Kate stood in front of Brawley's jail cell.

The man was sitting on his bunk, his head in his hands. After a moment he stood and faced her with a weary sigh. "What do you want? I thought I told you to stay away." His words came out in a growl.

She ignored it, smiled, and held up the ziplock bag of cookies. "I thought you might like some of these. Fresh-baked this morning."

He stared at her for a moment, then moved to the barrier between them and reached for the bag.

"Chocolate chip," she said and watched for the smile she hoped would come.

It was there. Almost.

He reached inside the bag and took out a cookie. He stared at it for a moment, then stuffed it back into the bag. She thought he was going to hand it back through the bars, but instead, he tossed it onto his cot.

Kate waited, shifting her weight from one foot to the other, then back again. She studied his profile and noticed the weary slump to his shoulders. "I've done a little sleuthing," she said. "It turns out you're from Copper Mill."

"What are you talking about?"

"You were quite the football star, homecoming king,

student body president . . . voted most likely to succeed in your senior class."

He raised his head and looked at her. "How did you find out?"

Bingo. It was the confirmation she needed.

"As I said, it was just some lucky digging. Several people in town thought they recognized you . . . A friend of mine started the ball rolling with an Internet search."

"So what are you going to do with the information?"

"I've already told the sheriff."

J.B. shrugged and looked away from her as if it didn't matter. But something in his eyes, just before he looked away, said it did.

She stood there for a few more minutes, then letting out her breath in a sigh, turned to leave. She wasn't sure what she had expected, but the awkward silence wasn't doing either of them any good. Plus, standing in one place so long was making her arthritic knee ache. She only hoped the cookies helped him understand that someone cared.

She had taken only a few steps when she heard him say, "Wait." She turned, breathed a prayer, then gave him an encouraging smile.

"Thanks," he mumbled. "For the cookies, I mean."

She nodded. "Chocolate chippers can solve a world of problems—or at least help ease the pain."

His face turned bitter again. "Not mine. But I appreciate the thought."

Kate stepped closer to the barrier between them. "What is it you're trying to solve?"

He let out a bitter laugh. "Oh boy. That's a good one.

I asked the deputy. I know who you are—the preacher's wife. It was your church I burned to the ground, and you've taken it upon yourself to help me solve my problems?" He laughed again, shaking his head. "I wouldn't blame you if you poisoned these cookies." Then he turned from her and half under his breath, added, "That'd probably be better for everybody."

Kate came another step closer. "Hey, buddy. First of all, I don't take kindly to your accusation. If I was going to snuff somebody out, I'd be a lot more creative than that—"

J.B. made a noise that sounded like a half chuckle, half sneeze. "Snuff somebody out?"

"Besides that, I wouldn't dare suggest that I could solve your problems." She held up her hands, palms out, and backed away from the bars. "You're the only one who can do that. Though from the way it looks right now, it seems like you'll be needing bigger help than what any human can offer."

"You probably mean the Big Guy." J.B.'s voice was heavy with sarcasm.

"I talk to him a lot. I'll mention your name." Again she turned to walk away.

"Mention my name?"

If she didn't know better, she would have thought he sounded disappointed. She swallowed a smile and looked back at him. "I'll do more than that if you give me the details. I like to know what I'm praying about." She narrowed her eyes, giving him The Look. It was a practiced expression that combined compassion with irritation, forgiveness with disappointment. She had used it often when her kids were teens. She was out of practice, but J.B. seemed to be paying attention. She added softly, "And I don't think it's about mercy and forgiveness for the fire."

J.B. blinked in surprise and rubbed his stubbled jaw. "You're saying that's an unforgivable offense?"

"No, I'm saying you didn't do it."

"Lady," he said wearily, "go back to whatever it is that preachers' wives do. What is it . . . put on teas and fashion shows for the wealthy so they'll give more money to your church?" He laughed; it was a mirthless sound. "Actually, that's not a bad idea. You'll need every penny to rebuild your church."

His cavalier attitude twisted her heart. The man was without conscience. She'd been wrong after all. "How did you know about that?"

"About what?"

"About the insurance?"

He looked genuinely puzzled. "What do you mean?"

She was weary of his game playing and shook her head slowly. "The lack of coverage," she said and headed for the heavy double doors. "I suppose Worldwide Destination Resorts did their homework, found out about the policy, and told you everything."

At the door, she reached for the buzzer as she called back to J.B. "One more thing . . . Just for the record, I don't snuff people out."

He didn't answer.

I pray for them, she added to herself. *Without ceasing. Details or not.*

IT WAS STILL DRIZZLING when Kate arrived home. She stifled a smile when she saw her husband holding an umbrella over little umpkins while he did his business by the maple tree.

He waved, then scooped up the Chihuahua, sheltering the little guy under his raincoat, and headed for the porch. Kate parked the car in the garage, then joined him.

"How's the babysitting going?"

He grinned as he held the door open for her. "All instructions followed to the letter. Medication. Trips outside. Even a delicious little scoop of ground steak, onions, and garlic."

"You're a good man, Paul Hanlon."

He put the dog down and helped Kate out of her coat. "But enough about Little Umpkins and me, how did the visit go for you?"

She sighed. "Oh, Paul. I'm so disappointed. I let my imagination get the best of me. I was so sure J.B. would open up—"

"And tell you he didn't do it?"

"Or that he was forced into it somehow. But he seemed more guilty than ever."

"Maybe we need to accept that he confessed because he did it, no matter the reason, and let the courts figure out the rest."

She smiled. "Thanks for not saying 'I told you so.'"

Paul had put together a small pot of minestrone soup out of leftover lasagna and served it to Kate with great fanfare. Soups and chili were his specialties, and it seemed he could throw together ingredients no one else would attempt. The results were heavenly. Who would have thought a can of kidney beans, a can of garbanzo beans, and a can of stewed tomatoes could meld together so well with leftover lasagna?

"Eli Weston called just after you left," he said after grace.

"The building contractor?"

"Used to be. He hurt his back, so he had to get out of the business. He runs an antique shop here in town now. From what everyone says, his input will be invaluable. He's stopping by later to let me know his thoughts." Paul scooped up a spoonful of minestrone. "We're blessed to have so many who want to help—from the pumpkin-show ladies to the building committee."

"Pumpkin-show ladies?" Kate grinned as she chased a piece of sausage around her bowl. "I think they'll like that. And there's already a building committee in place? That's great."

"I hadn't thought of getting a committee together, other than the church board, but Eli suggested it. He even said he would be happy to head it up."

"That is a blessing," Kate said. When Paul didn't respond, she studied his expression. "Something tells me you're not okay with all this."

He leaned back in his chair. "It hasn't even been a week since the fire, but the folks of Copper Mill are moving fast. Building committees forming, fund-raising efforts begun . . ." He shook his head slowly. "In San Antonio, this sort of thing would have taken weeks to get off the ground. It feels, well, uncomfortable somehow."

"Maybe it's simply because you've always liked to mull things over, Paul." She stood to clear the table. "Plan everything down to the wart on a gnat's knee before moving forward."

"But I want to make sure the plans are right," he said.

"And that God is in it," she added.

"Amen!"

ELI WESTON ARRIVED AT FIVE. She guessed him to be in his early thirties, younger than she expected.

"Please, come in," she said.

He stood there for a moment, staring down at Kisses, who was standing, ears back, beside Kate's ankle, growling. Kate took in Eli's husky build, shock of blond hair, brown eyes magnified by tortoiseshell glasses, and shy smile. She liked him before he said a word. Apparently, Kisses didn't.

"Hey, little tamale," Eli said. "You still mad at me?"

Eli knelt and reached out his hand. The Chihuahua tentatively moved toward him, more sideways than forward. Eli rubbed the dog behind his ears, then looked up at Kate. "This little brain packs a powerful punch for such a small body." He stood. "Renee stopped by the shop the other day to browse. I was leading her into the parlor to show her some really cool European crystal. Didn't realize the little dog was following me. I stepped backward and, well, oops . . ." He looked down at Kisses again and sighed. "My grandmother always said I was more a Joe Namath than a Mikhail Baryshnikov when it came to making my way through a room."

Kate grinned. "Don't be so hard on yourself. Joe Namath was pretty nimble in his day. Quarterbacks have to be."

He was looking at the Chihuahua again. "Anyway, bud. I'm sorry if I hurt you."

Kisses growled again and hid behind Kate's foot.

Kate laughed. "We're not going to let this little guard dog keep you out in the cold. Please, come in. How about some hot chocolate? Tea? Coffee?"

"You wouldn't happen to have a soda, would you?"

"Absolutely," Kate said.

He doffed his raincoat as Paul came up behind Kate. The men shook hands, and Kate hung the coat on the hall rack, then the three headed to the kitchen, followed by the Chihuahua.

Kate put a plate of cookies on the table, poured coffee, and grabbed a soda from the refrigerator.

Eli reached for a cookie and took a bite. After he complimented Kate on her baking skills, he said, "I realize you don't know me, so maybe I'm sticking my nose in where it doesn't belong." His big shoulders drooped, and the shy smile appeared again. "I'm not on the church board or anything. And truth be told, I haven't even been to services in a while, but I can't stand by and not at least offer to help. When I saw what happened to our church, well, words just can't describe . . ." His voice fell off.

"You have no idea what a gift your offer is—to the church and to me personally," Paul said. "Someone with your background will be a tremendous resource." He took a sip of his coffee and reached for a cookie himself.

"I'm not an expert," Eli said. "Far from it." Kate handed him the plate of cookies, and he took two. "I was in the construction business for four years. It was pretty cool. Loved the outdoors, the hard work. Thrived on it. Then a couple of things happened at the same time. My grandfather died and left me his home and business—Weston's Antiques. At first I was scared spitless. What was I going to do with a shop full of stuff I could break just by looking at it?" He laughed and reached for another cookie. "Not long after, I fell off a roof and twisted my back. Weston's Antiques became my saving grace."

"I think I've seen it on my way into town," Kate said. "An old house with a white picket fence. Is that it?"

The shop had intrigued her with its old-fashioned rocking chairs on the front porch, lace curtains in the windows, a water pump by the brick walkway, and scrolled gas street lamps flanking the front steps.

Eli smiled. "That's it. The house has been in the family for years. Belonged to my grandfather. It would have gone to my parents, but they moved away, so he decided to leave it to me." A shadow crossed his face, then quickly disappeared. "He died without knowing about my back injury, or that I appreciated his gift more than he could have imagined."

At Kate's feet, a sharp yip announced that someone was at the front door, even before the doorbell rang. The little dog took off so fast across the linoleum that he skidded into the refrigerator. But he was up in a shot and barked all the way to the foyer.

Kate knew before she opened the door that she would find Renee Lambert on the other side.

Renee stepped in, picked up the little dog, and hugged him close, murmuring something about "sweet little umpkins" and what a "big bad world" it could be when "mommy" wasn't near.

Kate was glad Paul wasn't within earshot; it would have been difficult to keep a straight face.

"Come in, come in," she said to Renee. "We're just having some coffee and cookies. Eli Weston is here."

Renee visibly shuddered at the word *coffee*. "Really, I thought I told you that it's terrible for the—"

"Oh yes, of course. Then how about some tea? I've cleared off the stovetop and found my teakettle."

"Eli Weston?"

"Yes, we're talking about the church. Come sit down with us. I made cook—"

"He nearly killed Kisses."

"He told us about the accident."

"I thought for sure his little foot was crushed. It broke my heart to hear him yelp the way he did." She shook her head. "It was terrible. He limped for days and still wakes up with nightmares."

Kate didn't ask how Renee knew what the little dog was dreaming about. "I'm sure Eli didn't mean to—"

"He should have taken greater care. There's no excuse. Distracted. He always seems distracted. And, really, I'm not so certain I can sit down at the same table with the man."

But she obviously didn't take her own threat seriously, because, chin in the air, she marched toward the kitchen. "I'll take that cup of tea," she said over her shoulder. "Earl Grey with natural sugar. Three cubes. And half-and-half, warmed."

She sat down with a heavy sigh, put her monogrammed Gucci tote on the table, then glared at Eli, who gave her a friendly smile in return.

The Chihuahua curled up by Eli's boot, put his chin on the toe, and whimpered. Bending over, he scooped up the little dog and held him close. Kisses licked Eli's cheek. Kate resisted exchanging a glance with Paul, who stood to serve more coffee.

"*Hunh!*" Renee said, her lips in a tight line.

PAUL AND KATE were getting ready for bed when the phone rang. Sitting on the edge of the mattress in his pajamas, Paul picked up the receiver.

"No, you didn't disturb us, Renee."

He listened for a few minutes, then said, "Thank you for telling me. I appreciate your thoughts."

When he hung up, he looked at Kate. "Well, that's interesting."

"What's that?"

"Renee called to tell me I've made a mistake."

"Dare I ask what now?" Kate said, rolling her eyes.

"She thinks Eli Weston shouldn't head up the building committee. She said he's had some legal battles over his inheritance as well as some other issues to deal with, though she didn't tell me what, and I didn't ask. He's distracted much of the time, according to Renee. Her proof? He stepped on little umpkins who was in plain sight."

Paul stood, walked over to the closet, and grabbed his robe. "She did say that if Eli can stop moping around, he might be up to the job."

"She actually thinks someone can do a good job?" *Wonder of wonders.* Though Kate bit her tongue and didn't say so. She was getting worried about how Renee Lambert seemed to have the innate ability to bring on these decidedly uncharitable responses. She quickly breathed a prayer for grace and promised herself she would be more careful.

Paul padded down the hall to the bathroom to brush his teeth. "No, she didn't say that exactly," he called over his shoulder. He stopped in the doorway and looked back. "You know Renee. The emphasis was definitely on the word *if*. If Eli gets over the moping, then he *might* be up to the job."

Moping? Kate certainly didn't detect any brooding behavior in the young man. He was reserved, perhaps a bit shy, but very sure of himself as he discussed the construction business with Paul. She admired that in someone so young. She could tell it was a career he loved and probably hated to leave.

She was sitting up in bed reading when Paul returned. "I was just thinking about Eli," she said as he slid under the covers. "Going from construction—enjoying the outdoors, doing hard manual labor, hands-on, rough-and-tough work—to selling delicate antiques had to have been quite a blow for him."

Paul reached for a book. "Serious back trouble would be hard for any young man to take. I think I'd mope too."

"Yet he's willing to endure what still must be a painful condition to help this little church in its time of need." She reached up to turn out her light. "Isn't it amazing how God uses the most unlikely of us—"

"To bring about his purpose," Paul said, closing his book.

Kate fell asleep thinking about God's grace, how he accepted her, warts and all, and how she needed to try harder to accept others, especially Renee Lambert. It seemed an impossible task.

Chapter Nine

The phone rang just as Kate finished her morning quiet time. She had been up since before dawn, unable to sleep, with a myriad of thoughts and concerns whirling through her mind. She knew from experience that her early mornings with God nourished her soul and gave her spirit rest.

The phone rang again. Paul was outside getting the morning paper, so she put aside her Bible, headed for the kitchen, and grabbed the receiver on the fourth ring.

"Kate, it's me," said a loud whisper. *Me?* Kate ran through the list of possibilities. Livvy's voice matched her petite size: bright, cheerful, and expressive. Renee's was low-pitched and raspy. LuAnne's was softly Southern and friendly, the kind of voice that sounded like she was smiling.

It was LuAnne. "Good morning," Kate said.

"They're here—at the diner!"

"Who?"

"The two men from that resort company—the ones I told you about."

"Oh yes, of course."

Paul came around the corner with the *Chronicle*. He grinned, gave her a quick good-morning kiss on the cheek, and tossed the paper on the table. He mimed "No coffee?" which she confirmed with a shake of the head. He pulled out the grinder and retrieved a bag of whole beans from the refrigerator. A whir followed, and a lovely fragrance wafted toward Kate.

"And just as we thought, they're up to no good."

"What have you found out?"

"Well, I'll get to that. But, darlin', I just know we're onto something. You should see how they're behavin'. Those two fat city-slicker felines look like they just swallowed a whole cageful of canaries." Kate could hear the clatter of dishes and utensils in the background. "Darlin', I'm gonna have to go. But I just wanted you to know what they said."

"You didn't tell me what they said."

"Oh, I didn't? Well, silly me. That was the main reason I called. One told the other he has an insider working with him to get the church land. Those were his exact words—'I've got an insider working with me.'"

Kate's heart twisted. "Who could it be?" And how could it be? How could someone from Copper Mill betray their community this way? Then she paused. "Maybe he meant an insider in some government agency, something like that. Not the community."

LuAnne chuckled. "Well, I could ask, but I don't think they'll tell me."

Kate hung up, then sat down across from Paul and told him what LuAnne had said.

His expression was grave, but it wasn't from her news. He handed her the newspaper. Across the top of page one, the two-inch headline read: ARSONIST'S IDENTITY DISCOVERED.

She skimmed the few paragraphs, then looked up at Paul. "They've used the same information Livvy and I found out. Nothing new."

He nodded. "What bothers me is that they're so hard on him. It doesn't matter about the brilliant, rising star he used to be. All that matters is what he did now."

She leaned in closer to the newspaper, examining the pictures reprinted from his high-school glory days, side by side with his mug shot. "What I wonder, Paul, is what happened during those years he was away from Copper Mill. Say he did start the fire. Why? Why would someone as bright and talented as he obviously was take this turn?" She poured coffee for them both.

"Maybe things didn't work out for him the way he thought they should. Sometimes that happens. Kids rise to stardom too early, especially if they're big fish in little ponds. They can never have that kind of adulation or glory again, and they end up bitter and disappointed, nursing a sense of failure because they can never achieve that sort of stardom again. They often blame everyone else, even God, for their own shortcomings."

Paul had a point. She thought about it for a moment, then said, "What about Worldwide Destination Resorts? Do you think there might be a connection?"

Paul nodded slowly. "J.B. doesn't really qualify as an 'insider,' but maybe there's someone else who then spotted him as someone to do his dirty work."

She shook her head. "It could have been the perfect

storm—the coming together of all the elements that make for disaster: J.B.'s anger, his need for money, the opportunity to get even with God." She paused, thinking through the possibilities. "I need to go back."

"To see J.B.?"

"I need to find out what happened during those missing years."

"Do you think he'll tell you?"

"No. That's why my first stop will be the library to do some more digging."

LIVVY WAS AT THE FRONT DESK when Kate arrived. She looked surprised to see Kate at the library so early.

"I'm in dire need of a high-speed Internet connection. Do you have a computer I can use?"

"*Mi casa es su casa*," Livvy said with a laugh. "And our computers too."

"We've got one, but by the time it hits a Web site, it's so slow I've forgotten what I was looking for."

"You're welcome to ours anytime."

As they climbed the stairs, Livvy explained the layout of the library. Kate could see the pride in Livvy's eyes as she pointed out their modern reference room, the nonfiction stacks, microfiche machines with old editions of the *Copper Mill Chronicle*, the collections of historical documents about the town, and a bank of high-speed computers.

Livvy left Kate sitting at the computer bank and headed back downstairs. Seconds later Kate typed in "J. B. Packer," then looked at the search results. One by one, she clicked the mouse on each link. The first four were real-estate agents, the fifth was someone looking for members of the same family tree. None of the next twenty-three looked promising, but she opened the sites anyway to see if there might be the slightest bit of information leading to Packer's whereabouts during the missing years.

Livvy reappeared at her elbow with two cups of coffee from the librarian's lounge. "Any luck?"

Kate shook her head. "Not so far." She clicked on the last listing and leaned closer. "Is this the Web site where you found the earlier info?"

Livvy looked over her shoulder. "No. This is different, but it's got some of the same information—his high-school achievements . . ." She paused, letting out a whistle. "And look at this . . . He was a national merit scholar. That's new information."

"And this." Kate's heart picked up rhythm as she read the heading: "J. B. Packer receives a four-year scholarship to . . ." The line broke off with a link to another Web site, where the article supposedly continued.

Only it didn't. She clicked on the link, and nothing happened. "Scholarship to where?" she wanted to shout. But instead, she counted to ten, went back to the original site, and read through the article again. This time she whistled. "Listen to this, Livvy. The gist of the article has to do with scouts from major colleges and universities around the country. On this particular night, which was an all-star game, scouts attending the game were from the University of Michigan, Ohio State, USC, and UCLA."

She grinned up at Livvy, who was still standing behind her, reading over her shoulder.

"How does this help?" Livvy asked, frowning.

"If he played ball for one of these schools, maybe his name will turn up in the archives of the school papers."

Livvy was grinning now. "You're good."

"You keep saying that, but this doesn't mean we'll get anywhere." She took a sip of coffee and went back to work. First she plugged in the information for the University of Michigan. Nothing. Then she tried Ohio State's the *Lantern*. Nothing there, either. Next was UCLA. Nothing. And finally USC. Her heart thumping, she waited while the *Daily Gamecock* searched for J. B. Packer.

Still nothing.

"Hey, girlfriend," Livvy said. "I've got to get back to work. I'll leave you to it. Call me if you need anything."

Kate was ready to shut down the computer when she decided to try one more source. Maybe major newspapers in those cities featured the new recruits. Local fans loved that sort of thing. Human-interest stories, the backgrounds of the kids arriving at training camp...

It was a shot in the dark, but she tried it anyway. Holding her breath, she typed in *"Los Angeles Times,"* clicked on the Web site, and keyed "J. B. Packer" into the search engine.

The little bar at the bottom of the screen shot little dashes back and forth, and the hourglass icon showed the search was in progress.

At least that was something. All the other tries had ended in three seconds or less.

Then articles and photographs materialized on her screen. Kate sat back, her heart thumping, her hands trembling as she moved the mouse to get the cursor out of the way.

First she studied the pictures. Two were the same ones Livvy had found. The third was a wedding picture. Standing beside Packer was his high-school sweetheart, Rachelle Kensington, in her wedding gown. The caption read: "Tragedy strikes fairy-tale couple, seen here in happier times." Next to that photograph was a snapshot of Packer, Rachelle, and a baby about six months old. This caption read: "Mother and infant killed by drunk driver: Husband and father, J. B. Packer." The final photo was of Packer receiving a medal of commendation from the Los Angeles fire chief, honoring him for his courageous actions that resulted in saving lives in a raging forest fire near Lake Arrowhead. The caption read: "From commendation to AWOL. No one knows the whereabouts of crack fire jumper since fiery accident took the lives of his family."

Tears stung Kate's throat, and she swallowed hard. The missing years. Now she knew.

She went back to the article and reread the final paragraphs, this time aloud:

> *Packer was cleared of manslaughter charges because he wasn't legally drunk. However, authorities say his consumption of alcohol was a contributing factor in the fiery accident that claimed the lives of his wife, Rachelle, and their baby daughter, Hannah Grace. This reporter traced this former hero-turned-tragic-figure to the area known as Skid Row in Los Angeles, where he is living and working as a janitor in the Union Rescue Mission under the fictitious name Jed Brawley.*

"I'm back." Kate stood outside J.B.'s cell.

When he looked up, she could see that his eyes were red-rimmed, the lines in his face deep. She pulled a bag of cookies out of her purse and handed it to him.

"Thanks," he said.

All the way to town hall, Kate had prayed for the right words to say to J.B. Now as she stood before him, words seemed inadequate. What could she say? The emotions were too complex, ran too deep. She remembered the words of Saint Francis of Assisi: "Preach Christ; if you must, use words." She hadn't come to preach, but she had come to reflect Christ's love to this prisoner. Maybe her presence was enough. Maybe she didn't need to worry about what to say.

"I just came from the library," she said.

"More digging, I suppose. I hope you're satisfied with what you found." He turned away from her.

"You've been waiting for the rest of the story to be discovered, then?"

"I figured the sheriff would be all over it like . . . never mind."

"You want to see what I found?" He turned, and she held out a copy of the *Times* article and photos.

"They got it right," J.B. said, his voice low. "All of it."

"About Rachelle and Hannah Grace?"

At the sound of their names, he looked up, tears in his eyes. "Yes. Everything."

A sting of tears crept to the back of her throat. She swallowed hard and blinked. "Oh, J.B., I'm so sorry."

A small flicker of a smile came to the corner of his mouth. "Call me Jed. I'm so used to it by now that J.B. sounds like someone else." He opened the baggie and grabbed a cookie. "These do help," he said. "Thank you."

"You didn't do it, did you?"

"Oh yes. We'd been out for pizza. I'd had a couple of beers, maybe more—there was a pitcher on the table. My reflexes weren't what they should've been. I didn't see the other car when I pulled onto the freeway." He looked away from her.

For a moment Kate didn't speak, then she said, "I meant the church fire, Jed. You didn't do it, did you?"

He stared at her. "I thought I did at first. That's why I confessed. I was nearby, saw the flames, the smoke, and ran to the church. Old instincts are hard to break. I wanted to help get anyone out who might've been inside." He dropped his head into his hands and rubbed his eyes. "That's when something snapped," he said, his shoulders trembling. "I opened the door and got hit by a wall of flames. I thought I saw Rachelle's face . . . the baby's . . ." His voice choked. "All I could think about was that it was my fault they died. The fire was my fault."

At the end of the corridor, the heavy door opened, and Skip Spencer stuck his head in. "Everything okay in here?" he called down to Kate.

Kate exchanged a glance with Jed, who nodded, then she called back. "Yes. Thank you."

"Alrightee, then. Just checking."

When the door slammed closed, Jed took a deep breath and began again. "I tried to get inside, but the wall of flames stopped me. Apparently I was running away from the church when the fire department got there. Saw me running; thought the obvious."

"You've got to tell them."

He shrugged. "Who's gonna believe me?"

"You've got to try."

He stared at her, unblinking, for several moments. The hollow look was gone, but in its place was too much pain and sorrow for one human being to bear. "You don't get it, do you?" His voice was husky with emotion.

She didn't speak.

"I deserve to be charged with this crime. Charged and sentenced and punished, just as I should have been when my family died."

"I'll tell the sheriff, then," Kate said, stepping closer to the bars.

"I'll deny everything I told you."

"They'll believe me. I'm the minister's wife."

He gave her a gentle smile, and she saw in his expression the man he used to be. "Yes, that you are. And my friend." He stepped toward her. "But I'll still deny it."

"What about the one who really did it? Can you let the courts prosecute the wrong man while the real criminal gets away?"

"Maybe it was an accident."

"I talked to the sheriff. It was no accident."

"I'm sorry, but I can't help you."

"I have to tell the sheriff what I found out."

He shrugged. "It doesn't make any difference to me."

THE SHERIFF WAS OUT, so Kate handed a copy of the *L.A. Times* article to Skip. "Make sure the sheriff gets it," she said.

But Skip's eyes were glued to the article, and he didn't seem to hear. All he said was "Whoa!" Then he let out a whistle between his teeth and said "Whoa!" again.

KATE STEPPED FROM THE TOWN HALL into the bright autumn sunlight, momentarily blinded. Then she saw the pink Sub-Zero parked next to her Honda and told herself not to groan.

Renee got out of her car as soon as she spotted Kate. "I finally figured out what you've been doing here. I brought you the first time, and you wouldn't tell me what you were up to. Then I saw your car parked here again . . . and then again, not more than a day or so later. I forget which day, but no matter—here you are again. And I'm sure it's to visit the perp." She stepped closer. "Am I right?"

Kate sighed and shot a prayer heavenward. "You're right, Renee. I did come to visit the prisoner. In Matthew, Jesus said—"

"What did you find out? I told you I was going to investigate on my own. You should have told me where you were going so we could share information. It's the only way we're going to keep the perp in the slammer. We've got to build the case against him."

"I think we're on opposite sides of this, Renee. I happen to think he's innocent."

Renee sputtered and didn't seem to be able to find the words to voice her dismay.

Kate decided to leave before Renee hit her with another lecture about seeing justice done.

"I must go, Renee. I'm sorry." Kate hit the UNLOCK button on her key ring, got in the car and pulled out of the parking lot. Then she stopped and looked back at Renee, who stood staring after her, looking terribly alone. And lonely.

She let her breath out on a sigh. *Okay, Lord, I know what you'd have me do. But I have to tell you, it's hard.* She laughed lightly as she backed up. "But you already knew that, didn't you?"

She pulled up beside the Oldsmobile, pushed the button on her door console, and lowered the driver's-side window. "Renee, how about coming by for some tea? I need to tell you what I've found out about the case. Maybe you can help me with some input."

Renee stared at her for a moment, then sniffed and checked her watch. "Well, I suppose I can squeeze it in. I've got an appointment in an hour."

"Wonderful. Would you like to ride with me? I can bring you back to your car later."

Renee reached in her car and retrieved Kisses, who wagged his tail when he spotted Kate. "Guess what, little umpkins," Renee cooed. "We're going to Grandma's house for tea."

Kate choked. *Grandma's house?* Renee was a good decade or two older than Kate. *Grandma?*

"Look at that, will you?" Renee climbed into the Honda and closed the door. Kisses scrambled to sit on Kate's lap beneath the steering wheel. "He's thrilled to be going back to the parsonage—aren't you, little umpkins."

Kate tried her best to keep her next thought from forming words, but they spilled out anyway: "How about if I babysit for little ump—ah . . . for Kisses while you go to your appointment?"

"How about that, punkin?" Renee said to the dog. "Grandma wants to babysit." She fixed a stare on Kate, then said, "Just because I'm letting my precious umpkins stay with you doesn't mean I'm not still upset."

"I understand," Kate said between clenched teeth.

OVER TEA RENEE READ the *Times* article. She blinked back
tears when she read about Rachelle and Hannah Grace, but
when Kate told her that Jed didn't set the church fire, she
said, "I don't believe him. I still think he's as guilty as dirt.
Besides, if he didn't do it, who did?"

"I don't know." Kate related what LuAnne overheard at the
diner.

"That woman is too nosy for her own good," Renee pro-
nounced, dismissing the information with a flutter of her
fingers.

Kate suspected that if Renee had been the one to garner
the same information, it would have been taken as gospel
truth and spread throughout the town as such.

Renee looked at her watch. "I must go. I really shouldn't
have let you talk me into leaving my car at the town hall. I'm
in a fine fix now, having to depend on you for a ride."

"It's not a problem," Kate said. Her jaw was beginning to
ache.

They stopped in the entry hall, and Kate helped Renee
into her faux leopard-skin jacket. Renee's attention seemed to
be caught by something in the large living room. She took a
step toward the doorway and stopped, staring at the sliding-
glass doors.

"Did anyone ever tell you those water spots look like a
flock of sheep?" she said.

A hint of a smile lit Renee's eyes. "Really, dear. You should
do something about this room." She rolled her eyes and
headed for the door.

"And while you drive me to my car, I'll tell you about Eli
Weston. I didn't want to go into the details with Pastor Paul

last night, but really, it's a story you should hear." She snapped the jeweled leash on Kisses.

Kate did her best to avoid gossip. She didn't spread it, and she didn't want to hear it. "I'm sure Eli will tell us what he wants us to know when the time is right." She opened the passenger-side door for Renee. Kisses hopped in with her.

"Fine. But he won't tell you. It's too terrible for him to talk about."

Chapter Ten

As soon as Kate dropped Renee and Kisses off at the town hall, she headed to the library only to find the parking spaces taken. It seemed Fridays were storytelling days for the little ones, because moms and preschoolers were streaming into the entrance.

Earlier Eli Weston had picked up Paul to take a look at some homes around the area that he had built before he injured his back. There was a cherry-pie special at the diner on Fridays, and Eli had suggested they stop in for pie and coffee before he dropped Paul back by the parsonage. That meant the car was Kate's all day. Paul's Lexus would arrive at the beginning of the following week, should all go well with the students' drive east, and she couldn't wait. She wasn't used to sharing a car.

At that thought she whispered a prayer for forgiveness. It seemed she was doing that a lot these days. And taking her blessings for granted was something she had to watch out for. So was complaining to God in the middle of the night because she was homesick for San Antonio. Many people had no transportation, or lived in their vehicles because they didn't have a home. She'd have to try to be more thankful.

She sighed. It was a good thing God loved her no matter her flaws, because it seemed that lately her flaws were becoming glaringly evident.

Kate found a parking spot a block away, and walked back to the library behind a mother with an infant in a stroller and a toddler by her side. Livvy had just stepped out of her office and was standing behind the front counter, sorting periodicals. She looked up and smiled as Kate approached.

"You've got that determined look in your eyes," Livvy said.

Kate lowered her voice. "Is there someplace we can talk privately?"

"We've got some private meeting rooms upstairs. Let's head up there." Livvy picked up the phone and asked someone to cover for her while she was in a meeting, then she led Kate into a small conference room behind the computers and closed the door. The women sat down across from each other at a long table in the center of the room.

"I was looking into Worldwide Destination Resorts," Livvy began.

"How far did you get?"

"Far enough to become alarmed, but it's going to take more sleuthing to find anything concrete."

"Like who the insider on this end is?" Kate said.

Livvy let out a sigh, and her disappointment was evident in her expression. "LuAnne called you this morning too?"

Kate nodded, then pulled out a pad and pen and settled back. "Tell me what you found out."

"For one thing, Worldwide has a bad reputation in the

industry. The company buys old hotels, renovates them, and turns them into upscale spas. I was able to get into the county real-estate transactions, deed records, and tax records." She leaned forward. "Listen to this: They've already purchased the Copper Creek Hotel, that run-down place next to the church."

"To renovate?"

"Yes. Big time. According to their Web site, the new inn will be up and running as a five-star, five-diamond destination hotel within the next twenty-four months. They showed prototypes on the Web, and I have to say, it is gorgeous. They're renaming it the Hamilton Springs Hotel. They show a two-story building where most of the rooms will be, then also a dozen or so private cottages around the property. The design, so they say, will ensure that all rooms have a view of Copper Mill Creek. The cottages will have wraparound decks overlooking the creek."

Kate looked up from her scribbled notes and tapped her chin with the end of her pen. "We're talking about adjoining properties. Let me guess, they want our land so they can expand."

"They *need* our land," Livvy said. "The cottages are all scattered over what is now the church property."

"They do this all the time, though. Wouldn't you think they'd have all their quails in a covey before embarking on a project this big?"

"There's another part of their story I haven't told you."

"Financial need."

Livvy grinned. "You've got it."

"Desperate times, you know, and all that. If they've

indeed gone this far without knowing they could get our church property—which is not a sound business decision, in my opinion—they're either inept and arrogant ...'"

"Or in deep financial difficulty," Livvy said. "And from other digging, it appears they're still trying to recover from other unwise investments. Their CEO was fired just six months ago, and a new one was brought in to turn things around. He's got a reputation for being pretty ruthless. Puts smaller hotels out of business just so he can come in and create a monopoly. That sort of thing."

"And then we have the bombshell LuAnne overheard this morning—the insider they're working with—which dovetails with what we've just uncovered. We've identified motive and opportunity, but we don't have any proof."

"We can guess what happened. They target Jed as someone in need of fast money—"

"He didn't do it," Kate said. "That's what I came over to tell you."

"Are up sure?" Livvy looked up at Kate in surprise. Kate nodded. "I talked with him this morning. He had some sort of flashback when he saw the flames. He confessed because he thought he had done it. Now he won't recant his earlier confession."

"Are you going to the sheriff with this?"

"I showed Skip the *Times* article, but Jed says he'll deny everything he told me." She sat back, tapping her pen on the pad. "The only way to see that justice is done is to find out who started the fire."

"Let me know what you'd like for me to do."

Kate stood and collected her things. "You've done so much already, Livvy. Thank you."

Livvy grinned as she pushed back her chair. "I'm happy to play Watson to your Sherlock anytime."

"Okay, Watson. Let's head to the computer bank. I'd like to take a look at some Web sites."

Kate opened the corporate Web site for Worldwide Destination Resorts. She was impressed with its high-end, glitzy look. Superficially, no one would know that this was a company in deep financial trouble. She surfed around to other related sites, then returned to WDR. A photograph of the new CEO, a balding silver-haired man with stark black eyebrows, stared back at her. He was dressed in an expensively cut suit and what looked like a silk tie. Next to his photo was a letter to shareholders listing upcoming ventures that would improve the solvency of the company. Topping the list was the Hamilton Springs Hotel and Spa.

She read through the connecting pages, but they told her nothing more than Livvy had related. She started to click the site closed, then at the bottom left of the page, she noticed a link she had overlooked: "Meet Our Family of Employees." She clicked on the fancy WDR 3-D logo beside it, and a page of employees' names came up, each with a thumbnail photo and brief biography. Another link led her to the site of recent retirees.

She spent several minutes scrolling through the list, not sure what she was looking for, then she reached for the mouse to close the site. But just before she hit the Close button, a photograph caught her attention.

She clicked on the image to enlarge it, then leaned toward the computer screen, squinting. She blinked, rummaged around in her handbag for her reading glasses, then looked again.

A sense of déjà vu drifted in and out of the edges of her mind. She knew this woman from someplace. But where? Her name and former position was given under the photo: Sybil Hudson, retired, administrative assistant to Charles Brandsmyth III, the former CEO. Her photograph showed her to be middle-aged, rather plain, and definitely no-nonsense. Her dark hair was slicked back, obviously caught up in some sort of bun or clasp, with straight bangs, and she wore small dark-rimmed glasses.

Kate was fairly certain she didn't know the woman personally, but rather, it seemed she might have seen her on television or in the newspaper. The nipping at the edges of her mind became clearer.

She pressed her lips together in concentration, then clicked on the search engine, typed in "Sybil Hudson," and waited.

Within thirty seconds, a list of Web site "hits" appeared, each having to do with Sybil Hudson. At the top of the list was an online journal, supposedly written by the woman herself.

Kate opened the blog and began to read. By the second entry, her hands were shaking, and a chill had spidered up her spine.

Heart thudding, Kate typed an e-mail to the address in the right-hand column.

Chapter Eleven

It was somewhere around one o'clock in the afternoon on Tuesday the following week that Kate decided to finish her pot-hanging project in the kitchen. She was expecting the Faith Briar ladies for a tea party on Saturday, and since inviting them on Sunday, she had worked as fast and energetically as her arthritic knee would allow, unpacking and tucking items away—from her large restaurant-sized mixer to her state-of-the-art food processor, her silver tea-and-coffee service to her best china and silverware.

There wasn't a moment while she worked that she didn't think about the mystery of the fire, or that chills didn't travel up her spine as she pondered a possible connection with Sybil Hudson.

Still thinking about the photo she had seen on the WDR Web site, she opened the box with her gleaming Mauviel copperware from Williams-Sonoma, pulled out the pots, and stacked them within reach on the counter. On Saturday, Paul and Eli Weston had hung an iron Tuscany-style pot rack above the counter. She had found it at Weston's Antiques, fallen in love with the rustic style, and though she had gone into Weston's with the intent of asking Eli about purchasing, or taking on consignment, the antiques that wouldn't fit in their house, she had purchased the pot rack on the spot. Eli had dropped it by personally that evening and insisted that he help Paul with the installation.

She had just climbed to the top of the ladder, S hooks in hand, when Paul, who had been putting tools away in the garage, raced through the front door.

"Guess what's coming down the street!"

She took one look at his face and knew. Paul's smile was as wide as she'd ever seen it, with the exception perhaps of their wedding day and the births of their three children. Kate carefully started back down the ladder. He caught her hand and helped her down the last few steps, and still holding hands, they hurried outside.

Paul's Lexus SC 400 had been a gift from Paul's uncle five years earlier. It didn't matter that it was already a decade old when he got it; the engine had hummed like a newborn kitten but had the power and speed of a cheetah in its prime. He babied the two-door coupe from the first night it spent in their garage, and not a week went by that he didn't wash and wax it by hand. Its original deep green paint still shone like a diamond.

David, one of the college students they had hired to drive the car to Copper Mill, had parked in front of the house, and his buddy, driving a beat-up nondescript SUV, pulled in behind him. The two climbed out of the vehicles, stretched, accepted cold drinks, then said their good-byes within the hour. They were obviously eager to be on their way back to San Antonio.

KATE HAD JUST FINISHED hanging the last of the pots and pans when Sam Gorman stopped by. Paul led him into the kitchen just as Kate stepped off the ladder. Without a word, the big man hefted the tall ladder with one hand and carried it to the garage for them. Paul and Kate smiled at each other.

He was back before they could say, "Good man to have around."

"I've been hearing rumors about your chocolate-chip cookies," Sam said. When he smiled, he again reminded Kate of a sea captain.

Kate laughed. "Made a fresh batch this morning. I was just about to ask if you'd like some."

Paul grinned. "I can always tell when Kate's puzzling something. She bakes. Usually cookies. It's her way of working through life's puzzles." He shot her an affectionate look.

"Life's puzzles?" Sam looked intrigued.

Kate placed the plate of cookies on the kitchen table. In little more than a week, they'd had coffee, tea, and cookies around that table with more members of their new congregation than she could count on both hands. She was glad this four-legged piece of Hanlon history was living on in Copper Mill as a place of counsel and fellowship. In San Antonio, the three Hanlon children had rolled out Play-Doh on its scarred surface when they were toddlers, then gathered for homework help when they were teens. The table had been the place where Kate had helped Melissa plan her wedding and where Rebecca told them she wanted to go to New York after college and try to make it on Broadway. It was also at this table that Andrew had opened the envelope giving them the news that he had passed the bar exam on his third try, and they all had wept with joy. The old table had seen Kate and Paul through Bible studies and prayers, times of sorrow and times of rejoicing. And now it had become the natural meeting place when members of their new congregation came to visit. Somehow, this little piece of home helped combat the waves of homesickness.

Kate sat down opposite the two men. "I suppose what Paul means is that I like to puzzle out things that intrigue me. Things that take hold of me and won't let go until I get to the heart of the matter." She laughed and reached for a cookie. "And whenever I'm puzzling something, turning different theories over in my mind, I bake. Mostly cookies. Especially chocolate chip."

"And I'm the happy beneficiary," Paul said. "Not only of the cookies but of her incredible insight from all that puzzling."

Kate laughed again. "Well, insight is one word for it. There've been times when I've missed the mark by a hundred miles. And Paul's being kind by not mentioning the times I was so caught up in puzzling things through that I forgot an ingredient or two. Like the sugar in my sugar cookies or the chocolate in my brownies."

"If these cookies mean you're working on something right now," Sam said, "I imagine we all know what it is."

"The church fire," Kate said quietly. "Usually I just think about little things that make me curious. But this . . . this is different. The church fire has to do with people's lives, with guilt and innocence, with heartbreaking loss and property damage." She paused, thinking about her involvement in the investigation. Until this moment she hadn't realized how strangely satisfying it was to probe for truth, no matter the obstacle. She blinked in awe as she realized that sleuthing was like a newly discovered gift, something that had been hidden within her until now—just when she needed it most.

"I happen to believe the man who confessed is innocent." She went on to tell Sam what Jed had told her.

When she had finished, he sat back thoughtfully. "So you think the only way to clear him is to find out who really did it."

She nodded, and Paul agreed. "Kate's already talked to the sheriff, who turned a deaf ear to the idea that someone else might be involved."

"I think Worldwide Destination Resorts might be involved," Kate said. "We all know they want our property. I mentioned it to Sheriff Roberts last week, and he almost laughed me out of the town hall. In essence, he told me not to worry my 'pretty little head' over the matter and to leave the sleuthing to the professionals."

"Funny you should mention WDR. That's one of the reasons I stopped by," Sam said. "The company somehow found out that Eli Weston is heading up the building committee and contacted him."

Kate's ears perked up. How would they know about Eli? Again, the thought of someone in Copper Mill working with the group chilled her.

Paul looked concerned. "What did they want?"

"They said they're willing to help Faith Briar with building plans, discounted construction materials, and financial incentives if we rebuild somewhere else. They thought by appealing to Eli as a builder, he could then convince the others on the committee and the church board to go along with the plan."

"Then plan to sell our property to them," Kate mused, feeling her cheeks warm. She considered Sybil Hudson's blog and what she had said about the other individuals and businesses rumored to have been stomped on, and worse, by WDR.

"That's right," Sam said. "That's just part of the offer. Apparently, they indicated they'd sweeten the pot even more should we sell."

"And if we don't?" Kate said.

Sam gave her a strange look. "They didn't say."

Paul was studying Sam as if puzzling something himself. He finally said, "I wonder why Eli didn't feel he could come to me with this information."

"Eli's tied up with a new shipment coming in from New Jersey and couldn't get away. I happened to stop by, he mentioned the contact, and I said I'd let you know. Needed to see Kate anyway about getting a choir started again."

Kate's heart dropped. She knew what was coming. Sometimes it seemed their house wasn't their own. Wednesday nights were slated for Bible study, Thursday nights for a men's prayer meeting, and now choir practice. Plus, the bell would be dropped into their backyard any day now, so there went the tiny garden of daffodil and tulip bulbs she had planned to plant for spring.

She let out her breath with a sigh. "And you need to meet here." Kate tried to keep a smile in her voice.

"Actually, no. Someone heard you sing and said you have a beautiful voice. Alto, I believe she said. I wanted to ask you to join us. We'll be meeting at Renee Lambert's tomorrow night."

"Renee Lambert? Is she in the choir?"

He shook his head. "No, but she's got a small organ. She called me this morning and offered her home for practice. And she's the one who told me about your voice."

Paul's smile was wide. "One thing I've noticed about this congregation is how everyone is sharing what they have to see us through—time, talent . . . such generosity."

Kate's voice was average. At best. But after what Paul just said, how could she say no? She wondered why Renee volunteered her organ, her home, and Kate's voice, for that matter. There had to be another motive . . . She halted midthought. Where was her charity, her grace, her unconditional acceptance of others? It was a good thing God wasn't finished with her yet. She had once seen a sign in a rather rambunctious Sunday-school classroom that warmed her heart: Be Patient with Us: Kids Under Construction. She needed a similar sign for herself: Be Patient with Me: Postmenopausal Woman Under Construction.

"What time?" she said to Sam.

"You'll do it? Six o'clock on the dot."

He reached for another cookie, then stood to leave. "By the way," he said. "Eli's been through a lot. This job is just what he needed to get active in church again, feel like he's one of us."

"That's what we understand," Paul said, walking him to the door. "I'm glad he's back. He's turned into my right-hand man. He's already found a company who'll haul away the debris at a discount. Plus, our first delivery of lumber is arriving tonight. It's too early to even think about building plans, but he found out about a liquidation sale at some big home-improvement company in Memphis. He said since the insurance money hasn't come in, he'll pay for it out of his own pocket. Get reimbursed later. Right now I don't know what I'd do without him."

"You know what happened, don't you?"

Kate gave him a puzzled look.

Sam swept back his hair with his fingers. He looked from Kate to Paul, then back again, and gave them a gentle smile. "Maybe it's better for Eli to tell you himself." He looked embarrassed. "I shouldn't have brought it up. I thought you knew."

Paul put his hand on Sam's shoulder. "He hasn't told us, but if he doesn't, that's okay too."

"Hey, Eli's a good man. To tell you the truth, I was worried about him. We all were. But we're seeing a new side of him, one that's been missing for months. And let me tell you, it's lightened all our hearts.

"Just like you said, Pastor Paul, God can give us joy instead of mourning. I've been praying that for Eli, and it looks like God has answered my prayer."

"Amen," Paul and Kate said together.

SKIP SPENCER WALKED with Kate down the corridor toward Jed's cell. "You sure come here a lot," he said. "You find out anything yet?" He looked so hopeful, as if he would give his right arm, maybe both arms, for the tiniest tidbit of information. Kate suspected he was desperate for a lead he could give the sheriff in exchange for a chance to get off desk duty.

There was something about Skip's expression that brought out the mother in her. She would love nothing more than to present him with the opportunity to crack the case. If she could ever convince Jed to tell the truth, she wanted Skip to be in on it.

"Nothing concrete," she said. "But if I do get the real scoop on something, you'll be the first to know."

His eyes lit up. "Really?"

"Really."

The young man whistled as he made his way back down the hall.

Jed was lying on his cot, his forearm covering his eyes. She thought he was sleeping and almost turned away, but he stopped her by sitting up and swinging his legs to the floor.

He moved slowly, as if his limbs were chained to the floor. She handed him the usual baggie of sweets—this time chocolate brownies—which he acknowledged with a nod. "The sentencing date has been set."

"I heard. Next week, isn't it?"

"Yes."

"I'm not going to argue with you about why you should tell the truth. You know my reasons. But I did want to leave you with something to consider."

He shrugged and sat down again on the cot, dropping his head into his hands. "Say whatever you want. You won't change my mind."

"You know, Jed, you can't do this on your own—starting with the barest essentials of forgiveness, mercy, and grace."

He looked up, his eyes red-rimmed, his complexion gray, his haggard face lined with deep crevices.

"No amount of self-punishment—including going to prison for a crime you didn't commit—will take the shame and guilt from you."

Jed's head had dropped again into his hands, his fingers splayed in his hair, his shoulders shaking.

"Only God can forgive what you think is unforgivable," she said. "And strange as it seems, he already has."

She waited to see if he would look up. He didn't. "One last thing," she said. "You won't be able to forgive yourself until you understand in your heart that you are forgiven. That God's grace is a gift, not earned."

She turned to leave, took a few steps, then turned back. "Oh, one last thing." She sighed. He lifted his head.

"The brownies I just gave you? I got busy thinking about this case, and, well, I think I may have forgotten to add the eggs. So if they seem a little flat and chewy, that's why."

Suddenly, he smiled, tears brimming. She saw a new emotion in his eyes. It was hope.

Chapter Twelve

The parsonage kitchen was so small, Kate and Paul did more than one quick dance step to avoid collision during dinner preparation. They were used to working together, but back in San Antonio, they hadn't needed traffic signals to open the refrigerator without bumping someone back into the entry hall.

Kate giggled the first three times Paul rounded the corner at the same time she bent over to grab a dish from the cupboard. The fourth time wasn't so funny. He was carrying a platter with a freshly grilled whole chicken from the outside grill when she backed into him, her arms full of salad ingredients. Paul gasped. She screeched. The chicken flew into the air. The head of iceberg lettuce bounced across the linoleum. Tomatoes and radishes rolled.

At the same time, Paul skated across the room, platter still in the palm of his hand, and somehow managed to rescue the flying bird before it hit the floor.

A twinkle in her eye, Kate quipped, "I guess we might say you caught a fowl."

Grinning, he set the platter on the counter and stooped to help her retrieve the vegetables. "And I guess you could say we already tossed the salad." They both laughed.

Their eyes met over the head of lettuce as he handed it to her. "You know, Katie, I don't think I've ever loved you more."

She tilted her head, enjoying the romantic look in his eyes. And trying not to think about the pain in her arthritic knee. "Even here in the middle of our tiny little kitchen?"

He helped her stand. "Especially here in our tiny little kitchen." He took in the worn linoleum, the oddly crooked painted cupboards, the old refrigerator with inner workings that sounded like a 747 racing down the runway. Then he met her gaze again. "You've given up so much. But I've never heard a word of complaint."

He didn't know she woke in the night, aching for home. Not for the material things. Truly, she was finding they didn't matter as much as she first thought they did. No, she ached for friends and family and, simply, the familiar surroundings of San Antonio where she had been born and raised. She ached for lost time, time alone when she could pursue her passion for her stained-glass artistry. But since they arrived, she hadn't found a spare minute to work on it—even if she had been able to find her boxes of supplies.

"I know this hasn't been easy," Paul said. "But I just wanted you to know how much it means to me—and how much I love you for it."

She smiled and touched his cheek. "As long as you keep catching those fowls and I keep tossing salads, we'll make a good team."

"Just as we always have," he said and kissed her.

It seemed they had been married forever, yet this man hadn't lost the ability to make her heart dance. She was still smiling as she placed the lettuce in a colander and turned on the water to rinse the leaves. Then she rinsed the tomatoes one at a time, dropping them into the colander with the lettuce.

"Sometimes I think about all we had at Riverbend and how easy something like this would be to handle. Not the emotional part—that would be devastating," Paul said. He picked up a tea towel, dried his hands, then slung it over his shoulder and leaned back against the counter. There was a half smile at the corner of his mouth. "But the financial struggles. There was a lot of money in that church. Wealthy donors who gave from the bottom of their hearts. Generous people who loved God and wanted to see his work go forward."

Kate tore the lettuce into bite-size chunks and dropped it into the spinner. "The church got whatever it wanted."

He nodded slowly. "That's it exactly. If we wanted a pipe organ, we got the best. Something that would fill that huge sanctuary and cause hearts to soar."

"Or if we started a building program," Kate added, "it was funded before the first bulldozer rumbled onto the site." She reached for the cutting board and a tomato.

"The biggest, the best—nothing stopped us from getting what we thought we needed," Paul reflected.

She tossed the chopped tomatoes into the salad bowl on top of the lettuce and reached for the radishes. "Does it bother you that we don't have the same donors here? That everyday seems to be a bigger struggle than the last? And that even now, we don't know if we'll have the money to rebuild?"

Paul studied the paint-splattered pattern on the linoleum for a moment before answering. "Honestly? Yeah. It weighs heavy on my heart. My prayer is that I'll know when the time comes how best to meet the challenge." His expression softened. "That I'll be up to it."

Kate put down the knife, wiped her hands, and reached for his hand. "I have no doubt about that, Paul. When God called you to this place, he knew what he was doing. He equipped you for this struggle. You will be up to the challenge—you *are* up to the challenge."

He reached for an avocado and cut it in two, pitted it, and as he sliced it over the salad, continued, "I could use a good dose of wisdom right now. You want to drive to Chattanooga with me tomorrow to visit Nehemiah?"

"As long as we're back in time for choir practice," she said, raising an eyebrow.

A hint of a smile returned. "Ah yes, choir practice at Renee's."

"I still wonder why she mentioned my voice to Sam."

"Because you have a pretty voice."

"Not that pretty. I croak on the high notes."

"That's why you're an alto."

"Middle C has even brought on a croak. I'll have to mime the words."

"Hey, you," he said, grinning. "There's another reason I love you."

"And that would be my creaky, squeaky voice?"

"No, it's because you're a good sport. You could have said no."

Kate took a deep breath. "The more I'm around our

parishioners, the more likely someone will slip and tell me something I need to know. Choir practice will be a good beginning."

They went back to work on dinner, still dance-stepping around each other. Paul carved the chicken while Kate whisked together an olive-oil-and-rice-vinegar dressing, then tossed the salad.

"About that organ," he said after a few minutes. "There are those odd little moments when I think, 'Boy, how I would love to add a pipe organ to the building plans.'"

"Somehow I knew the subject wasn't finished." Kate laughed and reached for the refrigerator door. He danced out of her way. "Or a big screen for projecting hymns and PowerPoint presentations?"

"Ah, you know me well."

"That I do, Pastor Hanlon. That I do." She gave him a kiss on the cheek. "And because you know me so well, you can guess what I'd like to do with the money we save by not putting your plan into action."

He popped a radish in his mouth. "*Hmmph*," he said as he chewed. "Has to do with cooking. Kitchen. Entertaining." He popped another radish.

"Close," she said. "Food, yes. Kitchen, yes. Entertaining . . . ?" She made a rocking gesture with her right hand. "Seriously, honey, I have a big dream for the church kitchen." She smiled. "Or maybe I should say a dream for a big kitchen."

"We've got to build everything exactly as it was. Eli has the blueprints from the old church. He knows an architect who'll update them once we get the go-ahead from the board. To keep the costs down, everything will stay the same."

"My dream has to do with a kitchen and fellowship hall big enough to supply meals for those who are having a hard time making ends meet and need a helping hand."

Paul's smile was soft. "I would love nothing better. It's a matter of money."

"And prayer," she added.

AFTER SUPPER KATE AND PAUL took the Lexus over to the site of the fire. As they drove by the creek, Kate could see beams from flashlights crisscrossing the church property and a few shadowy figures milling about. Apparently, word had spread about the lumber delivery. Who would have known the event would be such a draw? Kate laughed; she and Paul had come to watch just like everybody else. Were they already getting acclimated to small-town living?

Eli came over to greet them as they exited the car. He pointed with his flashlight beam to the lumber, which was stacked on what once was the parking lot. They followed him over to have a look. "High grade," Eli said proudly. "Redwood. Can't beat the price either."

The other shadowy figures materialized into Livvy and Danny Jenner, Joe Tucker, and Sam Gorman as they came closer to join the conversation.

"Did you hear about the latest offer for the property?" Livvy said to Kate.

Even in the dim ambient light of the flashlights, Kate could see the concern in her eyes. "I did," she said. "It gives one pause, doesn't it?"

Eli overheard the question. "They came to me. Practically offered us the sun and moon if we'd sell them this land." He paused, looking back toward the burned-out hulk where the church once stood. "I don't know how you all feel—and, of course, I can't make a decision on my own—but I'd like to tell them to go jump in the creek."

An almost imperceptible sadness crossed his face. It appeared then disappeared so quickly, Kate thought she had imagined it.

"I can't see putting up a new building anywhere but here," he continued. "I was raised in this church. Until the week he died, my grandfather rang the church bell every Sunday morning. No matter what. When he couldn't drive anymore, he walked, even in the snow. It just wouldn't seem right hearing that bell come from any other place but here by the creek."

"My gut reaction is to agree with you," Danny said, "but from a practical standpoint, we may not have a choice." He paused, looking every bit the professorial math teacher he was. His logic was right on target. Even so, something felt so wrong about it.

Paul turned to the others, stroking his chin, his expression thoughtful. "Sometimes we have to step out in faith," he said. "I know that financially we'd perhaps be better off selling this land to the developers, taking their money and rebuilding elsewhere. But in the short time Kate and I have been here, we've seen firsthand the incredibly strong faith of this congregation. We've also seen what this place—not just the building but the setting, the land, even the creek view—means to each individual and family. In some cases, generations of the same family have worshipped here.

"When you consider the births, deaths, marriages, anniversary celebrations through the decades—and yes, even

Eli's grandfather ringing the bell—you can only conclude that this very ground is sacred."

Silence fell. Kate looked around in wonder. The rushing sound of the creek carried like music toward them on an almost balmy Indian-summer breeze. *Sacred? Oh yes.* Kate's eyes stung with tears.

Paul continued, "I think about those first members of Faith Briar and the sacrifices they made to put up a building here. I've been doing some research at the library, pulling up old microfiche accounts. I found out that this core group of only seven or eight miners scraped together all they had—and in some cases, it was little more than a widow's mite—and they bought this land.

"These were men with families, and obligations that go with them. But they gave of their time and money because they knew it was what God wanted them to do. Their children needed a Sunday school. Their wives needed a place of worship. These men stood before God and said, in essence, 'Hey, we're your guys.'"

He grinned. "They arrived here, where we're standing, before they reported to the mine—no small feat, because their workday started at dawn. And they came back at night after their shifts were over, mining lamps attached to their caps so they could see to work after sundown.

"I think about the dream they had for this holy ground, I think about how hard they worked to fulfill that dream, and honestly, folks, I can't imagine building anywhere else."

There were murmurs of agreement.

Danny cleared his throat. "I say we spread the word," he

said. "We'll rebuild right here, no matter what it takes. No matter how long. No matter the sacrifice."

Paul's gaze met Kate's. She saw compassion, commitment, and wisdom in his eyes, and though it was difficult to tell in the dark, she thought she saw tears. She thought about how far they had come—from the comforts of San Antonio and the large congregation that wanted for nothing to this place of sacrifice. They had so little to work with, yet never had God's grace seemed so abundant.

"Amen," she whispered.

THERE WAS A MESSAGE on their answering machine when they arrived home. It was Skip Spencer. He sounded excited. "Missus Hanlon," he said. "The arsonist wants to talk to you again. He said to call and tell you he's ready to talk."

"Do you mind going to Chattanooga alone?" Kate asked Paul a few minutes later. "I should go see Jed first thing in the morning."

"I agree. Do you want me to come with you?"

She shook her head. "He might not open up if someone else is there. But I do want him to meet you as soon as possible."

THE PHONE RANG in the middle of the night. Kate squinted at her bedside clock: 1:46. She reached for the phone, hoping it wasn't an emergency with one of the children.

"Mrs. Hanlon?"

"Yes," she said groggily.

"It's Eli."

"Oh yes. Eli. What's wrong?"

"Can I talk to Pastor Paul?" He sounded frantic. "Please. And fast."

"Of course." Frowning, she handed the receiver to Paul.

He listened for a moment, then said, "Eli, it's okay. It's a setback, but we'll recover. God won't abandon us now."

Paul fell silent again as the young man went on. Then he said, "Call your contacts in the morning. See if they have any way of tracing the shipment. Find out when we can place another order."

He paused, listening, then said, "The bulldozer?"

The two men talked for another few minutes, then Paul returned the receiver to the cradle. He swept his fingers through his hair, then let out a deep sigh.

"We've had some vandalism," he said. "The entire shipment of lumber was stolen tonight. And the bulldozer's gone. Eli is frantic. The dozer, as he calls it, belonged to a friend."

"Oh, Paul," Kate said, reaching for his hand. "What next?"

Chapter Thirteen

Time crawled after Paul left for Chattanooga. Three times Kate started for the front door, and three times she was called back by a ringing phone. She was tempted to let it ring through to the answering machine but worried it might be an emergency, so she reluctantly headed back to the kitchen each time.

The first call was from Renee Lambert asking if she could drop Kisses by for a visit to "Grandma's" that afternoon. Annoyed, Kate prayed for grace, which took longer than usual to find its way into her heart. So while she waited, she prayed that she would at least see the humor in the grandma bit. It came faster than grace did.

"Bring Kisses a sweater," Kate said. "I'll take him with me on my afternoon errands."

Renee seemed stunned that Kate so readily agreed. "All right," she said. "But if it starts to rain, I don't want him to leave the house."

"Bring an umbrella," Kate said between clenched teeth. *And make sure it matches the sweater.* She added a request for forgiveness to the prayer she had just shot heavenward.

The second phone call was from Livvy, who had done more digging on the former CEO of Worldwide Destination Resorts. "He died just a few days ago," she said. "His vehicle went off a cliff in the San Bernardino Mountains of California. The weather was clear and warm, and there wasn't much traffic. There's an investigation."

Kate promised she would stop by later so they could do more surfing for clues on the Internet. She also wanted to check her e-mail to see if she had heard from the CEO's former administrative assistant, Sybil Hudson.

The third call was from LuAnne, who had made great strides in finding volunteers to head up the pumpkin-festival committees. "Listen to who I got," she said, her words coming out in a hurried whoosh. "Betty Anderson. Have you met her yet, darlin'? She's the proprietor of the beauty shop. She's planning to talk up the pie-baking contest and can't wait to enter it herself.

"Then there's Phoebe West—I think I told you about her new baby. Cute as a bug's ear. Name's Violet. Same as her eyes. Anyway, she said she would be in charge of the Little Miss Pumpkin contest."

LuAnne was on a roll. She barely stopped to take a breath. "We'll have an auction. People are plannin' to bring apple butter, jams 'n' jellies, fudge, and . . . oh my, I get hungry just thinkin' about it. Can you imagine all this comin' together the way it has? It's a God thing, though I'd love to take credit for it!"

Finally she stopped to catch her breath, and Kate broke in with a laugh. "You've done an incredible job, LuAnne."

LuAnne laughed. "That's my policy, darlin'. If there's a job that needs doin', do it right, I always say. Otherwise, don't bother at all."

"Maybe we can talk to the other women about it at the tea on Saturday. You'll be there, won't you?"

"I wouldn't miss your tea for all the tea in China." LuAnne chuckled. "It'll be a good time to enlist the help of the church ladies. Everyone I've talked to says they can't wait to come to Kate Hanlon's fancy tea party."

"Fancy tea party?"

"That's what they're saying."

"Oh dear. I don't want people to think it's anything out of the ordinary. I just wanted to do something nice to get to know the women in our congregation."

"Honey, don't worry about that. The ladies of Copper Mill are ready for 'out of the ordinary.' You're from the city, and we're all dying to see how you do things. We've all heard about the smart way you've hung your pots, and we can't wait to see it."

Something about it all was unsettling to Kate. Being talked about behind her back was bad enough, but having something she considered a labor of love put down as a means of putting on airs twisted her heart. She wondered who first dubbed it her "fancy tea party." She had a pretty good idea.

IT WAS AFTER TEN by the time Kate got to the town hall. "I may need you as a witness later," she said to Skip Spencer when she checked in. "Bring a tape recorder, pen, and pad." She was guessing at what the legalities might be in this case, but figured it wouldn't hurt to at least start here—and at the same time, give Skip a bit of the glory—then let the sheriff take over.

Skip blushed the hue of his hair, and his eyes brightened. "Wow," he said. "You bet!" He opened the heavy double doors behind his desk, and she stepped into the corridor leading to Jed's cell.

"You wanted to see me?" she said to Jed a moment later.

He stood and walked over to the bars between them. "You were right," he said quietly. "I need to tell the truth."

She let her breath out slowly. "You're doing the right thing."

"That doesn't mean they'll believe me."

"They may not. But it's a start."

"It probably means I'll go to trial . . ."

"And you're worried about representation?"

He nodded. "I'm not sure what the courts provide."

"We'll face that later. Besides, I happen to know a very fine attorney."

"I don't have any money," he said.

"It's my son. He might be able to help—at least get us in touch with someone here who can."

"I don't know where to start."

"At the beginning," she said gently. "Tell me everything. I've asked the deputy to join us with a tape recorder. Is that all right with you?"

He nodded.

Two hours later, the deed was done. Skip Spencer performed admirably, for the most part keeping silent, and once in a while asking questions for clarification. Mostly, Jed just talked into the mike. He told about the past, his sorrow over the deaths of his wife and daughter, the misplaced guilt when he ran into the church and faced the flames.

Skip turned off the recorder and, shoulders back, headed back down the hall. He was whistling a Disney tune, appropriately, "Whistle While You Work." Kate prayed the young man wouldn't somehow inadvertently erase the tape.

Then she looked back to Jed, whose face was gray with fatigue. "Are you going to be okay?"

"I'm tired. Bone tired. But in some strange way, the darkness that's usually in my head isn't there. I can't say I'm out of the woods. I've got a long way to go"—his smile was faint—"but the guilt that's been hanging around my neck for so long doesn't feel like the Rock of Gibraltar anymore."

"The way God works within us—to change our hearts, to heal our grief and sorrows, to strengthen us—isn't a one-time event," Kate said. "Nearly always, at least for me, it's a process."

"A journey," he said. "I sort of figured that. And I've got a long way to go."

"But you've taken some important first steps."

They talked for a few minutes about the next steps in the legal process and what he might expect.

"My husband and I are here for you," she said before turning to leave. "Call us anytime."

"There's something else," Jed said, frowning. "It may be nothing. But the morning of the fire? I thought I saw someone leaving the church. It wasn't anyone I recognized. Just a figure."

Kate's breath had caught in her throat. She stepped closer to the iron bars. "Male or female?"

He shook his head. "Male, I think. But I couldn't be certain. It didn't come to me until I was going over the events just now with the deputy. I didn't say anything because I wanted to make sure I really saw something. After changing my story once . . ." His voice drifted off, and he shrugged. "The only image that's clear is that the person was wearing a hat."

"A hat? What kind? Can you describe it?"

"It was a baseball cap. Dark, maybe black. It had a white logo on the front." He shrugged. "I'm sorry. That's about it."

"Do you think you might recognize the logo if I brought some samples in?"

"I didn't get close enough to it. I only know it was dark with a whitish logo." He frowned. "There was something else about it, though. The iridescent white seemed to have eyes, like it was an animal of some sort."

"What kind of animal?"

"I don't know. And maybe it was just my imagination. I flipped out around that time."

"Do you think the person saw you?"

"No. I'm almost certain I was hidden from view."

"You should have said something about this to the deputy."

He shook his head. "He'd thought I was making it up . . . trying to pin the arson on someone else."

"Is there anything else you remember? Facial features . . . length of hair, clothing, coat?"

He shook his head. "Just the baseball cap. Sorry."

RENEE AND KISSES DROVE UP in the Oldsmobile at the same time Kate headed the Honda into the garage. She gritted her teeth, preparing for the word *Grandma*, as Renee and Kisses exited their car, but it didn't come. As requested, Renee had dressed the Chihuahua in a bright pink sweater and brought along a matching umbrella in the event the misty drizzle turned to rain. A tiny satin bow was Scotch-taped to the top of the little dog's head.

Within a few minutes, Renee had fluttered her fingers, blew a kiss to "sweet umpkins" and slid back into the Oldsmobile.

"Well, now," Kate said to the dog, who looked up at her with that familiar doleful expression. "I guess you and Grandma are about to make a day of it." She followed Kisses to the maple tree and held the umbrella in place, taking greater care to keep sweet umpkins dry than to keep her own hair from frizzing.

When Kisses finished his doggy business she led him into the house, checked the answering machine, then grabbed her raincoat. Five minutes later they were on their way to the library, Kisses on Kate's lap, nose pressed to the window.

The drizzle was turning into a serious rain, so Kate tucked Kisses underneath her raincoat, then headed into the library. "You've probably got rules about this sort of thing," she said to Livvy and opened her coat enough to reveal the Chihuahua's pointed nose, dark marble-sized eyes, and floppy ears.

"Ah, babysitting, I see."

Kate sighed. "I don't know how it happened, but I'm suddenly little umpkin's grandma. It's becoming a regular thing. Renee seems always to have some appointment or another."

She bit her tongue to keep from adding that the appointments were probably for taking care of her roots and getting a massage, facial, manicure, or pedicure.

Livvy shook her head in sympathy. "Most people tell her no. You're kind to agree to it." She scratched Kisses on the head. "Actually, on a day like today, you can just keep him tucked in your coat. If you were babysitting a Saint Bernard, it would be a different story."

They headed upstairs to the computers. While Livvy pulled up the information on Charles Brandsmyth III, Kate checked her e-mail.

She had two messages. The first was from Sybil Hudson. She clicked open the body of the letter.

Dear Mrs. Hanlon,

I will be happy to talk with you about my former employer, Worldwide Destination Resorts. Unfortunately, a dear friend and my former boss died just three days ago, and I must fly to California for the funeral. If you will be so kind as to send me your telephone number, I will call when I return. Electronic correspondence is not a secure way to communicate, and I must warn you, if you are investigating WDR, your life may be in danger. Watch every move you make.

Sincerely,
Sybil Hudson

Kate printed out the letter and handed it to Livvy. "Do you think she knows what she's talking about?"

Livvy shook her head slowly. "It sounds like she's either a

disgruntled employee trying to get even for real or imagined wrongs, or she's the real deal and this company is bad news."

"Everything we've seen so far points to some sort of a bully mentality, and there are hints of unethical practices. But no charges have been made, no arrests." Kate sat back staring at the screen.

"There's the CEO's death in California."

"Why would they want to get rid of him? He wasn't an enemy."

Livvy shrugged. "Maybe he knew too much. Plus, his administrative assistant called him her dear friend. If they were close, he may have been about to tell all. Somebody found out and did him in."

"That's true," Kate said. "The big question is if they're involved in anything underhanded here. You heard about the vandalism last night?"

"Yeah. Eli called Danny. I heard this morning that they found the bulldozer. Someone drove it off a cliff above the creek. It didn't go in the water, so the sheriff will be able to dust it for prints."

"Eli felt terrible about it. He's taking all this so personally."

"We all are."

Kate started to open the second e-mail, but Livvy said, "Here's the latest from the *L.A. Times* about the accident investigation."

Kate adjusted her reading glasses, leaned toward Livvy's screen, and began to read. In her lap, Kisses had started to snore.

"Don't tell me that noise is coming from that tiny Chihuahua nose," Livvy said.

Kate smiled. "It can get worse."

The *Times* article didn't report anything new about the investigation, but an eyewitness had come forward to say he saw a logging truck tailgating the CEO's Hummer minutes before it went over the side of the cliff.

"Jury's still out on this one," Livvy said, shutting down her computer.

Kate started to do the same, then remembered she hadn't read the second e-mail. She moved the mouse to click it open.

She sat there in stunned silence.

"What's wrong?"

Kate pointed to the screen.

Livvy frowned, then leaned over Kate's shoulder to read the e-mail. "There's no return address. Or name. Or anything." When Kate didn't say anything, she frowned. "Are you okay?"

Kate licked her lips and finally said, "Who would send a death threat to a minister's wife?"

Chapter Fourteen

K ate was sitting by the fireplace in her bathrobe reading when Paul got back from Chattanooga.

"How was your visit?" she called to him as he hung up his raincoat.

He poked his head around the corner on his way to the kitchen. "A day with Nehemiah was just the tonic I needed." Then he came back to sit beside her in front of the fire. He looked more relaxed than when he left.

"He sent me home with something for you. He fixed chili, his special, one-of-a-kind pumpkin chili."

"Seventy-nine years old, and he cooks a pot of chili while you're visiting?"

Paul grinned. "And with flair. You should have seen him. He whirled around that little kitchenette like it was Emeril Lagasse's personal workspace. He'd invited me to have dinner with him in the Orchard Hill dining room, but after I told him about the pumpkin festival, he couldn't wait to pull out his special recipe and show it off. He thought maybe we could use it at the festival. He sent the recipe home with me."

She reached for Paul's hand. "Tell me what Nehemiah said about our troubles here."

He squeezed her fingers and seemed to be studying her expression. "Before I get started, tell me about your day. Is everything okay? How was choir practice?"

She thought about it for a minute but didn't know where to start, so she said, "I think we need Nehemiah's wisdom as a foundation before we launch into my day."

"Was it the meeting with Jed? He changed his mind about talking?"

"Actually, that was one of the high points of my day." She smiled so he wouldn't worry. "First, tell me about Nehemiah."

"I had no more than walked in the door when he opened his Bible to Second Corinthians and read chapter four. He seemed so excited, he could hardly sit still. This morning, when he was praying for us—all of us . . . Faith Briar, you and me—he thought about the passage. He says it's a promise to cling to during these difficult days."

Paul got up and retrieved *The Message* from the lamp table by Kate's rocker. He thumbed to the New Testament, found the passage in Second Corinthians and began to read aloud:

> *We're not giving up. How could we! Even though on the outside it often looks like things are falling apart on us, on the inside, where God is making new life, not a day goes by without his unfolding grace.*

"He agrees with us about rebuilding on the present site, no matter the cost. But he also cautioned me to remember that the church isn't a building. It's the people, God's people, who make up his church."

Paul stood up to stoke the fire. Sparks flew upward, crackled, and sizzled. After he sat down again, he said, "When I told him about the latest—last night's vandalism—he told me something that I hope I never forget." He paused, still watching the fire. "He said that without life's challenges, we won't see God's grace at work. We won't see the unfolding of miracles. Or God's transforming power."

He turned back to Kate. "I don't know about you, but I needed that reminder right now."

She took a deep breath. "Amen to that."

"Now for your day."

"I'll start with choir practice at Renee's—I actually had a lovely time. Renee served dessert—apparently cakes and pies are her specialty. The evening turned out to be a nice break from the rest of my day. I'm ashamed I grumbled so much about having to go."

Paul raised a brow. "And about the rest of your day . . . ?"

Kate filled him in on the details about her meeting with Jed and his decision to tell the truth, the deposition he gave to the sheriff's deputy, and the flicker of hope she saw in his eyes.

"After that, I babysat Kisses, which wasn't so bad, but I cringe every time Renee calls me Kisses' grandma."

Paul rolled his eyes. "And you said it went downhill from there? That's bad enough."

She leaned forward and took his hand again. "I had a death threat."

"What?" Paul was on his feet before the word had left his mouth. "A what?"

"A death threat. Someone threatened my life in an e-mail."

"Who was it—or do you know? Was there a return address, a name, anything?"

She shook her head. "Nothing. After I got home, I called the sheriff. He couldn't come, but he sent Skip over to talk to me, get a copy of the e-mail for their records."

"Does he know anything about Internet security, how something like this might be traced?"

"He's pretty computer literate, from what I could tell, but he couldn't figure it out either. They're sending someone over to the library tomorrow to check the computer program I was using. That may give them some clues."

She went into the kitchen for the e-mail and brought it back to Paul. It took him less than ten seconds to read the three sentences:

Mrs. Hanlon, I know who you are and where you live. Keep your nose out of things that are none of your business or you will be sorry. Your life is in danger.

Paul frowned, reread the note, then looked up at Kate. His eyes were sad. "This is serious. Kate, please promise me you'll stop this investigation. It isn't worth it."

"I know it's serious, Paul, but I'm not going to stop looking into the church fire." She laughed lightly. "In fact, it just makes me all the more determined to find out who did it and why."

He sighed. "I know I can't tell you what to do, Katie, but please be careful. Will you at least promise me that?"

Kate nodded.

"Do you have any more leads?" he asked.

She shook her head. "All signs point to WDR." She told him about the e-mail from Sybil Hudson. "They play dirty from everything I've read. This note might be just a sampling from their bag of tricks."

"I worry about you, Katie. The quicker I can find out who's behind the fire, the safer we'll all be." She gave him a soft smile. "But I promise to pay close attention to where I go, when, and all that. Do the buddy-system thing."

Paul sighed. "I know you. Once you get it in your head that something needs doing, you throw caution to the wind. That's why I worry."

PAUL SNORED LIGHTLY beside her, but Kate couldn't sleep. She flipped her pillow over three times, adjusted her position, thought about counting the flock of sheep on the sliding-glass door, worried over her arthritic knee, then flipped her pillow again. Her mind whirled with thoughts of the fire, WDR, the stolen lumber, Jed, the pumpkin festival, rebuilding worries, then back to the fire again.

The clock in the entry hall chimed one o'clock, then two. Sometime before three, she finally drifted off.

Then, suddenly, she woke with a start and sat up in bed. It was as if a flash of lightning had struck her. Her mind raced along almost faster than she could keep up with it.

The baseball cap! She had seen something like it before! But where? When?

She pictured it as Jed must have seen it. Dark background. Some sort of iridescent logo above the bill. It wasn't much, but it was something.

She fell asleep again, and when she woke at five thirty, she wondered if she really had seen the cap before, or if it had just been a dream.

Chapter Fifteen

K ate spent all day Friday washing and ironing table linens, polishing silver, and shopping for exotic teas and whole-bean coffees. She pulled out her recipe book and settled on her favorite finger sandwiches—tiny cream puffs filled with a variety of chicken, egg, and crab salads. She also decided on a mixed green salad with toasted pine nuts, dried cranberries, feta cheese, and a dressing of balsamic vinegar and extra-virgin olive oil, with a hint of crushed garlic and fresh ground pepper.

Paul and Danny borrowed folding tables from the Presbyterian church and set them up in the living room. Later that evening LuAnne and Livvy stopped by to help set the tables with Kate's ivory tablecloths and matching napkins, her grandmother's antique china—supplemented with an inexpensive silver-rimmed set—and centerpieces of chrysanthemums and fall foliage.

Kate pulled out her teapot collection, remembering the friend or family member who gave each one to her, and placed them on the tables. There were elegant pots, tall and stately; cute little squatty pots; some with whimsical artwork; and even one that was designed to look like it was upside down. Kate loved them all, mostly because they reminded her of the one who gave it to her. She especially adored her mother's silver teapot, given to her mother and father on their silver anniversary.

When the decorating was complete, she stood back to survey the room. Even with the dark paneling, oversized fireplace, and the flock of milky sheep on the slider, the room was beautiful. Who would have thought she would someday have her own tearoom? It was another of God's little unexpected blessings. She smiled at the whimsical thought.

SATURDAY MORNING dawned bright and beautiful. At seven thirty, Paul gave her a quick kiss and left to go fishing with Eli and Sam.

At precisely 9:58, everything was ready. By 10:23, Livvy and LuAnne had arrived to help, and by 10:39, the doorbell started ringing.

Faith Briar ladies of all ages, shapes, and sizes poured through the front door wearing their tea-party best, some with hats and gloves. Renee made her usual splashy entrance with Kisses in her arms. She wore a wide-brimmed hat with a froth of pink silk roses that matched her Laura Ashley rose-print dress, white gloves, and strappy heels. She fluttered her fingers, took over conversations, and made her rounds as if in charge of the tea.

Kate told herself not to be bothered by Renee's behavior and concentrated instead on the laughter and happy chatter that soon filled the little parsonage.

The women obviously knew each other well. *Another advantage of small-town living*, Kate thought. She could hear snatches of conversation about children and grandchildren and friends who had moved away. Of course, the ladies of Riverbend Community knew each other and chatted about the same things, but this seemed, well, different. It seemed like family.

Livvy caught Kate's hand and squeezed it. "This is wonderful, Kate!" She gestured to the living room, where the ladies were taking their seats at the tables. "We've so needed something special to get our minds off the fire."

Kate made her way to the front of the room and smiled at the little gathering. "Welcome," she said. "It's wonderful to see you all here. I've met some of you before today, and others for the first time, but I'm hoping we can all get better acquainted during this time of fellowship and fun. This tea party is simply my way of saying thank you for making me feel so welcome in your community—and in the Faith Briar family.

"Let's ask God's blessing on this occasion and on the food," she said. "Then let the tea party begin!"

THE DAINTY FINGER SANDWICHES were passed around, tea poured, salad served. Fresh fruit and crème fraîche and petits fours.

The conversation turned naturally to the pumpkin festival with dozens of questions and comments and ideas being tossed back and forth among the tables. While Livvy then LuAnne gave the women the latest details, Kate and Phoebe took out fresh trays of the tiny puff sandwiches and served each table. The excitement seemed to grow as the women talked about sewing projects and baked goods they could sell.

The auction seemed of special interest, and as Kate poured fresh tea from her mother's silver teapot at each table, the women peppered LuAnne with questions.

Livvy, who was helping Kate pour tea, sidled closer. "I've just had a brainstorm," she whispered. "Why don't you show the ladies one of your stained-glass pieces?"

The light dawned, and Kate smiled. "To get a buzz going for the auction?"

"How about the piece you showed me yesterday—the Tiffany-style lamp? Would you mind showing it? It might trigger some ideas. We've got other artists at Faith Briar. Phoebe paints with watercolors, Abby does ceramics. Maybe yours will encourage them."

Livvy clinked her water glass with her spoon. "Ladies, we have a treat in store today. I've just asked Kate to show us the stained-glass piece she's planning to donate for the auction. She doesn't talk much about it, and she certainly doesn't know I planned to say anything about her artistry today, but her artwork is exactly what we're talking about that will bring in the kind of money we need to rebuild Faith Briar."

"I'll be happy to donate it," Kate said. "Working with stained glass is a passion of mine, but since we moved, there just hasn't been time. I'm hoping to get started again soon. I'd planned to put up one of my pieces for auction, but I couldn't make up my mind which one"—she grinned at her friend—"until Livvy here mentioned the lamp."

Kate stepped into the spare bedroom. Her supplies were still in boxes, but a few of her favorite pieces were on a high shelf in the closet. She opened the closet door, reached for the heavy table lamp, and held it close, almost as she would have a baby. How could she part with it? It was the last piece she made in San Antonio, in the studio she missed terribly and would never see, or use, again. A touch of homesickness nipped at her heart.

But the lamp would bring in more money than any of her other pieces of art. Hugging it close, she turned to go back into the living room.

She had almost reached the doorway but was still hidden from view, when she heard Renee's voice.

Her breath caught in her throat as she listened.

". . . and I don't mean to criticize, but really, pots and pans hanging from the ceiling like she's some sort of TV chef? And the antique china . . . and the silver? It's Gorham, you know. Albemarle, and at least a hundred years old. Sterling. It must have cost a fortune. I can only imagine how the money could have gone to better use, like feeding the poor or something . . . Putting on airs, that's what she's doing. Trying to show us mountain women how highfalutin entertaining should be done."

Kate halted midstep and frowned. Surely she wasn't hearing correctly. The hairs on the back of her neck stood up straight; her cheeks turned warm. She counted to ten and ordered her feet to stay put, then took a deep cleansing breath.

It didn't help. She increased the count to twenty and considered other options: locking herself in the bathroom, leaping out a window, tearing into the living room and confronting Renee.

All three were appealing. With a deep sigh, she dismissed them all.

Instead, she put her shoulders back and shot another prayer heavenward. Her prayer list was getting longer by the day: Grace, forgiveness, humor, and now strength and a healthy dose of patience.

She plastered a smile on her face and rounded the corner into the tearoom.

"Ah, there she is." Livvy's voice was unnaturally bright. "We were getting worried. And there's that beautiful lamp."

The women were subdued as they gathered around to examine her artistry. Kate did her best to keep the atmosphere upbeat, light, and joyful, and to keep from glaring at Renee. It was a struggle.

After Renee's tirade and the resulting subdued mood, Kate expected the ladies to leave early, but surprisingly, most seemed genuinely reluctant to say good-bye. She was relieved when Renee excused herself, saying she needed to get Kisses home for his nap.

The atmosphere brightened considerably once Renee left. At least a dozen women stayed to help with cleanup. Millie, the church secretary with a vibrant smile, trotted to the sink and started rinsing the china.

"Honey, I love these dishes," she said. "I just bet they were your grandma's—or someone else special like that."

Kate could have kissed her. She grinned. "Yes, they were. I treasure them. I use them for special occasions."

"And the silver service?"

"A gift to my parents from their friends on their silver anniversary."

"I thought so," Millie said with a wink. "I think we all figured that."

Livvy, LuAnne, and a handful of other ladies who had been working around the kitchen stopped to listen. A few others drifted in from the living room where they had been clearing the tables.

There were murmurs of understanding, words of support for Kate and Paul, and mentions of how glad they were to have them as part of the community. The ladies' expressions of compassion and their gestures of love spoke louder than words.

Abby Pippins came over and gave Kate a hug. "We all figured you overheard the mean things that were said. But you need to know that Renee doesn't speak for the rest of us."

Kate took a deep breath. "Thank you all for staying to help, but more than that, thank you for understanding." She paused. "Honestly, I thought the day was ruined. But your love—a reflection of God's own—has done much to help me through a difficult day. Thank you from the bottom of my heart."

LuAnne had tears in her eyes as she made her way through the tangle of women to stand by Kate. "This here is one classy lady," she said to the others. "She's worked tirelessly to put this tea together, and let me tell you, she's diggin' in scary places to see that justice is done in this arson case. And at great personal cost."

She looked over at Kate. "Darlin', can I tell them about the death threat?"

Almost as one, the women gasped.

"Death threat?" Abby said and put her hand to her rather ample bosom. "Oh my."

"Like on TV?" Dotty wanted to know.

"Absolutely," LuAnne said. "And is she gonna stop pokin' her nose into this business? You can bet your sweet bippy she's not. This lady is as smart as a whip, as brave as a mountain lion, and as sleuthy as Miss Marple."

"As a what?" Dotty asked, cupping her ear. "A marble?"

"Miss Marple," LuAnne said a little louder. "Miss Marple."

Kate grinned and hugged LuAnne. Smart, brave, and sleuthy. Never mind that sleuthy wasn't really a word. All in all, it wasn't a bad image.

THAT NIGHT, KATE SAT ALONE by the fire, reflecting on the day. Her feelings were mixed. It had ended well, but she was still disturbed about Renee's comments.

She examined her own heart, wondering what God was trying to teach her in this. Had her actions triggered Renee's words? Was there any truth to the accusation that she was putting on airs?

In this little town, would it have been better to have put together a simpler gathering? Did it really offend Renee—or any of the ladies—that Kate seemed to have blown in from the city with her gourmet recipes, fancy cookware, and fine china? Did they feel she was trying to show them how things *really* should be done? Did they really think she was putting on airs?

She had told herself she wanted to put on the tea as a gift to Faith Briar in this desperate time of need. But in reality— and it hurt her to even consider it—had she wanted to show off her skills, her pretty dishes, her flair for cooking?

Was Renee right?

She bowed her head. *Oh my, Lord! I prayed that you would refine me, that you would help me simplify my life, but I didn't expect it to hurt so much. Help me do what I know must be done.*

Paul was already asleep when she crawled into bed. She turned out her light, and lay there in the darkness, staring at the ceiling. Her knee ached from all the activity of the day. But it didn't hurt half as much as her heart did.

Chapter Sixteen

K ate pulled up in front of Renee's house at 8:15 Monday morning. She had called earlier to ask if she could stop by. Renee had sounded hesitant but finally said yes, albeit with an annoyed sigh.

Renee was waiting for her at the front door with the Chihuahua in her arms. Dark circles ringed her eyes, and rather than her usual morning designer warm-ups, she had on a worn duster and house shoes.

"Thank you for seeing me," Kate said. "I think it's important."

Renee stood back so she could enter, fluttering her fingers as if Kate's visit meant nothing.

Renee led Kate into the small, beautifully designed living room that Kate had seen from the entry hall on the night she came to choir practice. Now that she got a closer look, she was taken by the decor. The colors were mostly mauve, ivory, and pale green. If Renee designed it herself, she did a magnificent job. She told Renee so.

Renee sat down heavily without responding. Kisses hopped into her lap, circled around until he was comfortable, and began to snore. "It's awfully early for a social visit," Renee said.

"I want to talk to you about Saturday."

Renee gave her a sharp look. "About what?"

"About what you said when I was out of the room . . ."

"I suppose someone told you. I should have known. And I'm sure they embellished—"

"I heard what you said. Every word. I was standing in the hall."

"About your china and silver?"

"Yes."

"I didn't mean for you to overhear," she said quietly and let her gaze drift away from Kate's face.

"I do wish you hadn't said what you did to my guests," Kate said. "It wasn't the time or the place."

Renee jumped to her feet. The Chihuahua snorted and landed by her ankle, blinking his eyes. "I should have known you came here to chew me out. You should have warned me. I'm just not up to this today. I wouldn't have agreed."

Kate stood and said, "Let me finish. I didn't come here because I'm angry with you."

Renee picked up the little dog and let out a sigh. "Okay, let's hear it. You may not be angry, but I'm sure you've got something unpleasant on your agenda."

"I wanted to apologize to you, Renee. That's why I'm here."

"Apologize?"

"You were wrong about the china and silver and the implication that I spent too much money on them. They were gifts from my family—inherited. I enjoy using them because Paul and I never would have been able to afford anything that nice."

"I'm sorry," Renee mumbled, embarrassed. "I didn't know."

"But what you said about putting on airs . . ."

Renee let her gaze drift again, and her cheeks turned pink. "I don't know what got into me . . ."

"No. Let me finish. You were right about that."

"What?" she almost croaked.

"For a long time, I've been praying that God would help me simplify my life. When Paul and I decided to move here, I prayed even harder that God would show me exactly what that means." She paused. "There's nothing wrong in putting on a fancy tea for the people you love. But if you're trying to impress them with your finery or cooking skills, well, that's not right."

Renee was gaping at her as if unable to believe her eyes . . . and ears.

"You told the women I was putting on airs."

Renee swallowed hard. "I-I shouldn't have done that. I was mad about the arsonist. I'd had a call the night before from my neighbor Lola. She heard it from her sister Maude, who heard it from Skip Spencer, who said you'd been to the jail, advising Jed to renege on his confession. I was spitting mad, if you know what I mean. Remember what I said about justice being done? Well, I haven't changed my mind. He's as guilty as dirt."

"I don't think he did it," Kate said gently. "And the sooner the sheriff and everyone else understand that, the sooner we can find the real arsonist."

"Sit down." Renee fluttered her fingers toward the chairs they had just vacated, then added, "Please."

Kate sat, and this time Kisses hopped onto her lap, circled a couple of times, then settled down to sleep.

"Tell me, who's the perp if it isn't the guy who's in the pokey."

Pokey? Kate stifled a smile, then she told Renee about everything, including the ominous e-mail threat.

"A death threat?" Renee sounded impressed. "Really?"

"Whoever sent it must believe I'm onto something, or they wouldn't have bothered. That gives me hope that I'm getting close to discovering who did it."

Renee bit her lip and nodded slowly. "Aren't you worried?"

"A little. But I plan to be careful."

"You'll need to BOLO."

Kate frowned. "BOLO?"

"That's police lingo for 'be on the lookout.'"

"Of course, I didn't know."

"You need someone to watch your back." The look on her face said she wanted to sign up for the job.

Kate studied the little woman sitting in front of her. Whether she was wearing a worn housedress and slippers, a faux leopard-skin coat and spike heels, or a straw hat covered with roses, Kate couldn't imagine for a moment that she could watch someone's back. But the image did make her smile. Again. Maybe all those prayers for grace were beginning to be answered.

"You want a job?"

Renee's eyes lit up. "Really?"

"I need someone to, well, go over details with and ... ah ... get input on ideas I have for ... um ... finding the arsonist." She was making it up as she went along, but the look on Renee's face was worth it.

"I watch *Law and Order* reruns every night, so I know the drill. I know how to nail those perps."

"*Hmm*," Kate said. "That's great."

"I'm sorry I got so mad," Renee said, her raspy voice almost a whisper. "I don't know what got into me. And I shouldn't have said those things at the party. Can you forgive me?" She blinked rapidly as if to keep tears from puddling.

"You didn't even need to ask," Kate said. "It was done before I got here."

"Would you like some . . . ah . . . coffee?"

"You have some in the house?"

Renee gave her a half smile. "I keep some in the freezer in case a friend stops by."

"I would love some. Just black, please."

While Renee was in the kitchen, Kate picked up a stack of three magazines from the coffee table. Two were put out by the American Kennel Club, and the third was called *TEACUP*, specifically for owners of miniature dogs. On its cover was a fancy teapot, circled by a half-dozen teacups, each with a miniature Chihuahua sitting inside, looking out at the world with big soulful eyes.

Kisses still snoring in her lap, Kate thumbed to the cover article: "Ten Ways to Build Self-esteem in Teacup Chihuahuas." She read the first two tips:

1. Give your pet a dignified name. Don't be tempted to be cutesy just because your dog is small. His or her ego is at stake. Your intonation when you speak your pet's name can make or break his or her self-image. Suggested names for teacups are Gerard for a male or Genevieve for a female.

2. Don't use baby talk when speaking to your pet. Your intonation as you speak these cutesy endearments can make a little dog feel even smaller . . .

Renee bustled back into the room, carrying a mug of coffee for Kate. She looked down at the magazine in Kate's hands.

"It will be hard to give up calling him little umpkins," she sighed. "And I adore dressing him in pink, but I may have to give that up too."

She went back to the kitchen and returned a minute later with a cup of Earl Grey and three cubes of natural sugar for herself and a plateful of cookies for them both. She sat down opposite Kate and glanced down at the magazine, now back in place on the coffee table.

"I don't think you've got anything to worry about. Little um . . . ah . . . Kisses seems to have quite a nice ego. You can tell by how he wags his tail and perks up his ears."

"I would agree with you, except that after Eli Weston stepped on him, he slunk around here on his belly for days. It really scared him. I don't think Kisses knew how small he was until then."

"He seems to have recovered. You're not thinking of changing his name, are you?"

Renee fluttered her fingers. "Oh goodness, no. Talk about an identity crisis." She took a sip of tea. "Speaking of Eli— he's found a crane operator to deliver the bell. It will arrive tomorrow."

Kate's sip of coffee went down her windpipe. "Tomorrow?" she sputtered.

"Bright and early. I plan to come over and take pictures of the crane lifting it in."

Kate told herself not to think about the bell swinging over their house and what might happen if a cable slipped.

"It's broken my heart to see it covered with mud and ashes and broken pieces of charred steeple." Renee had tears in her eyes. "It's the one thing in that little church that remains solid and sure. If that bell could talk, think about the tales it could tell." She paused for a moment. "My own wed—" She caught herself and stopped abruptly. "I mean, the weddings, the funerals, the births . . . the bell tolled for each." She blinked rapidly, then took another sip of tea. "My goodness, the stories . . ."

"No one else thought to do anything about it," Kate said quietly. "It will mean a lot to everyone once they see what you've done."

"Plus, it's one more way to keep Eli busy," she said with another flutter of her fingers. "We've all been so glad to see him finally getting back to living again. He dragged around town something awful for months after his fiancée was diagnosed with cancer. Then after she died, he seemed, well, so distracted by his grief, and he was driving the rest of the town nuts."

"I'm so sorry. I didn't know. Several have mentioned his recent troubles, but not anything specific."

"He's been so sad, he wouldn't leave his quarters above the shop. And he kept the shop closed for weeks on end. And then, as I mentioned, the—"

"Yes, distraction. Now I know why everyone is so pleased to see him working on rebuilding the church. It's given him a new lease on life." Kate took a final sip of her coffee, gently placed Kisses on the floor, and stood. "I really need to be on my way, Renee. Thank you for the coffee—and for the visit."

"Don't forget about the bell," Renee called after Kate as Kate headed to her car. "And maybe you ought to think about cleaning it up before services on Sunday. You could probably pick up some special metal polish at the hardware store."

Kate counted to ten, then turned back around with a smile. "How about if we work on it together?"

"Oh, I'm sorry. I have a nail appointment right after I stop by to see if the bell arrives safely."

RENEE OCCUPIED Kate's thoughts as she drove home. She was a proud woman. Kate had already noticed that she attempted to shave years off her age, dressed like someone at least two decades younger, and sent a not-so-subtle message with the ever-present Youth-Dew.

Kate turned the Honda from Ashland onto Smoky Mountain Road, pulled over, and bowed her head.

How easy it is to misjudge others, Father. Forgive me. Even if I'm wrong about this, I have no right to judge her. She took a deep breath. *And Lord? Thanks for being patient with me. This refining business isn't easy. Will I ever learn?*

AFTER AN AFTERNOON of running errands—a trip to the grocery store and the cleaners, and a quick stop at the library to visit with Livvy—Kate had just pulled into the garage when Eli drove up and parked in front of the house.

She greeted him with a wave as he trotted up the sidewalk toward her.

He smiled. "Greetings, Mrs. Hanlon. Is the pastor home?"

"His car is in the garage, so I think he is."

"That Lexus is sure a beauty," he said as they walked toward the door. "I can see why he takes such good care of it."

Kate laughed. "Sometimes I think he loves it as much as one of our kids."

Eli looked shocked.

"I'm kidding, of course."

He gave her another of his shy smiles. "I knew that."

They entered the house, and Eli went with Paul into the living room while Kate headed to the kitchen to start dinner.

She dumped chopped onions and garlic into a gleaming copper frying pan with a drizzle of olive oil. The scent drew the men like a magnet, just as Kate knew it would. There wasn't room for all three in the small kitchen so Paul and Eli plopped down at the table.

"We're having spaghetti tonight," she said to Eli. "How about joining us?" She opened a package of spicy pork sausage and broke it apart into the pan. The browning crumbles sizzled and danced in the skillet as she chased them around with a fork.

"Hey, cool. I'd love to."

She opened two cans of tomatoes and a can of tomato paste, dumped them into a separate pot at the back of the stove, then reached for some dried oregano.

"Can I set the table?" Eli looked happier than she'd seen him since the day they arrived.

"Absolutely." She stepped out of his way and pointed him in the direction of the flatware and everyday dishes. "And the napkins are in the pantry closet."

"You've got a pantry?"

She laughed. "It's makeshift. Try the little cupboard over the fridge."

Paul grabbed the lettuce and tomatoes from the refrigerator, snatched the colander, and turned on the faucet.

"Hey, this is really cool," Eli said. "It reminds me of being with my grandparents when I was a kid. I was there more than I was at home."

He must have noticed something in Kate's expression, because he quickly added, "I don't mean you look like them. They were pretty old. I don't know *how* old, but they seemed old . . . I mean they weren't *really* old, just—"

Paul jumped in to ease the young man's discomfort. "Katie, did you know that Eli and I both attended East Tennessee State?"

Eli shot him an appreciative grin. "That almost makes me family, right?"

It melted her heart. Having Eli around was like having one of the kids home again.

They had just finished dinner when the phone rang.

Kate picked it up at the same time Eli and Paul got up to clear the table.

"Missus Hanlon?"

"Yes?"

"This is Skip Spencer, down at the station?"

"Hello, Skip."

"I've got big news I thought you'd want to know . . ."

Behind her, the clink of dishes being rinsed and the whoosh of running water made it difficult to hear. She signaled Paul, who turned off the faucet.

"Tell me again, Skip. I'm sorry, I couldn't hear you."

"I was saying that the sheriff says he doesn't have enough evidence to keep J. B. Packer, especially because of that death threat you got. He thinks there's somethin' else going on here. Plans to release Packer Wednesday morning. I just thought you'd want to know."

"That's great news. I appreciate you telling me."

"And Missus Hanlon? There's something else."

Kate drew in a deep breath. Sometimes it took Skip forever to get to the point. "What is it?"

"The prisoner, J. B. Packer? Well, he remembered something else about the fire. He says it's important."

"Did he tell you what it is?"

"No. He says he needs to talk to you. He asked if you could come to the town hall Wednesday when he's released. He'll tell you then."

"Of course. I'll be there."

"He's getting out at ten."

Kate hung up and punched the air with her fist. "Yes!" She

laughed. "Hallelujah and amen!" She felt like dancing around the kitchen, arthritic knee and all.

Paul looked over from the sink, soapy plate in hand. "What's going on?"

"Jed Packer is being released. The sheriff decided there wasn't enough evidence to tie him to the crime. Can you believe it?"

Paul's smile was as wide as Kate's. "Thanks to you, Katie, an innocent man will not be prosecuted." He crossed the room and gave her a hug. She loved how he smelled of lemony dish soap.

Over her husband's shoulder, Kate smiled at Eli. The young man looked uncomfortable and let his gaze drift away from hers.

Her heart went out to him. Their open show of affection couldn't help but bring back the acute memory of his loss.

Chapter Seventeen

The phone rang at 6:37 the following morning. Kate set aside her Bible, trotted to the kitchen, and caught it on the fourth ring, just before it clicked over to the answering machine.

"Is this Kate Hanlon?"

"Yes, it is."

"This is Sybil Hudson. You contacted me about Worldwide Destination Resorts?"

"I'm so glad to hear from you. Yes, I did contact you. I've been concerned about your safety since you left for California."

There was a moment of surprised silence, then Sybil said, "That's sweet of you to worry. And honestly, I don't know how far WDR would go to cover their tracks in my case—or in yours. Or how far they would go to scare you off—if you are who you say you are."

Kate frowned. "Who I say I am?"

There was a moment of silence. "I'm sorry," Sybil said, "but I'm a little uncomfortable with this—and I know I'm coming across as a little paranoid. But believe me, I've got good reason to be." She paused, and Kate could hear the kitchen clock ticking. "After all, I don't know you from Adam."

Kate sighed. "I guess you have no way of knowing. If you'd rather meet with me in person, maybe we can arrange that, though I don't know how that would convince you either." She sighed again. "All I can say is that I'm a pastor's wife in Copper Mill, Tennessee." She explained about the fire on their arrival day and about the arrest of a man she didn't think was responsible. "I've got references," she said, "if you need someone to vouch for me . . ."

Sybil laughed. "You sound as honest as the day is long. Besides, who would lie about being a pastor's wife? My dad was a minister. My mom still says that being a preacher's wife is one of the hardest jobs there is."

Kate laughed lightly. "What can you tell me about WDR's plans for Copper Mill?" She pulled out a scratch pad and pencil from the drawer below the phone, then sat down at the kitchen table.

"I was still with the company when it was in the earliest development stages. Management's motives were great, and they were actually planning to do what they do best—take an old run-down property and restore it to its original glory.

"Then reports began to leak out that top management was involved in illegal practices—mostly stock manipulation, insider trading, that sort of thing. Just the rumors of it caused the stock to drop to the point that the whole company was in peril.

"The investigation is still ongoing, and nothing has been

proved, no charges filed. Just innuendo. But the damage has been done.

"That's when things got dirty. The company needed a scapegoat to reassure the shareholders that everything was in apple-pie order. They picked my boss . . ."

"Charles Brandsmyth III," Kate filled in.

"Yes."

"He was forced to retire?"

"It was either that or they said they would go public with their accusations that he was behind the leak to the media about insider trading, that he was the ringleader and in fact encouraged his cronies to sell before the big news hit about a disastrous project on the California coast."

"Was any of it true?"

"He was behind the leak. I know that for a fact."

"Because he had you make the call."

She laughed. "You're quick. But it wasn't a phone call. I met with a reporter friend of mine and told her what was going on."

"And the other, the insider trading?"

"No. Not an element of truth to that accusation. They were just trying to scare him into leaving. Of course, once he retired, they leaked plenty of 'hints' of impropriety, insinuating that the bad apple was gone and the company could turn itself around."

"That's when you retired."

"Right again. I couldn't stomach the smear campaign. The sad thing is, most of the company is filled with good, honest people, true believers in what they're doing. Rather than tearing down old, often historic, buildings and putting up new ones, they restore them to their original glory. Better than original, because they put in all the modern conveniences of today's world. Have you heard of Spain's paradors?"

"No."

"The government takes centuries-old castles, manor houses, and the like and turns them into four- and five-star hotels. They're beautiful and they preserve history. That's the kind of thing WDR wants to do, and has done so well in the past."

"It sounds like you still believe in the company."

"I do. I just hope someone can root out the *real* bad apples."

Silence fell between them for a moment, then Kate asked, "Is there any evidence of foul play regarding your boss's accident?"

"None that can be proved." Her voice sounded incredibly sad. "I can't believe anyone at WDR would go that far, but as I've said on my blog, things have gotten so bad, they may do anything to try to hang on to their power. People send me nasty e-mails saying I'm either making it up or I'm paranoid.

"Charles was writing a book, an exposé of illegal practices not just by WDR but by other corporations recently in the news."

"And you think," Kate said, "that word got out about the exposé and someone had him run off the road."

"That's what I think, but I can't prove it."

"What about Copper Mill? Is there anything you can tell me that will shed some light on what's going on here?"

"You mean, do I think they would burn down a church to get your property?"

"Yes. Exactly that."

Sybil let out a deep sigh. "A year ago I would have said absolutely not. But now I have to believe that they may be capable of such an act."

Kate tapped the eraser end of her pencil on the table. "You said you were still working for them when they purchased the Copper Creek Hotel."

"Yes. I remember it well. Charles actually put them onto the place. His people came from around there. His roots were still in the Tennessee hill country. He came back often to fish, though he mostly kept to himself. He loved the small-town atmosphere. That tells you something about the man's heart. Though he was the CEO of a multibillion-dollar company, lived in a New York penthouse, and was driven everywhere by a chauffeur, he never got caught up in the trappings of power and wealth." She chuckled. "He once showed me a photograph of himself standing by his Jeep near his favorite fishing spot in Copper Mill. You wouldn't have known it was the same man." She paused, and her voice choked when she continued. "I'd never seen him look happier."

"It sounds like you loved him," Kate said quietly.

"I did, but not in the way people might think. He was my friend. That's why I can't let go of what happened to him. I want to clear his name, honor his memory." She fell silent again, then added, "And if possible—and I don't know how, because I don't have any pull in the company anymore—see that the hotel gets renovated and lives up to his dream."

"But with a church next door."

Sybil laughed. "Absolutely."

Before they hung up, Sybil said, "I warned you by e-mail

a few days ago, but I need to tell you again—watch your back, Kate. If, in fact, WDR was behind Charles's accident, that means they've upped the stakes, and you're no longer safe in your own home."

She told Sybil about the threatening e-mail. "What I don't understand is how they knew I was nosing around."

"I would guess it was because of your e-mail to me. But don't blame yourself. Though the post was supposedly private, any hacker worth his salt could get into my system and find it—and many others—if he wanted to. When you post something on the Internet, you might as well figure you're skywriting. If people know where to look, they'll find it."

THE FLATBED TRUCK with the crane roared up the street at 7:57 AM. Behind the truck was another with the church bell sitting muddy but proud in the bed. Leading the parade was the pink Oldsmobile with Renee behind the wheel, Kisses in her lap. Eli Weston brought up the rear.

As soon as she parked, Renee leaned out the window and waved merrily to Kate and Paul, who stood on the front porch. Then she jumped out of the car, Kisses on his jeweled leash, and raced across the yard to tell Eli and the crane driver exactly how she wanted the bell placed.

For the next half hour, the men talked about how best to lift the bell over the roof and swing it into the backyard. At first Eli thought they might have to cut down the maple tree to get it to fit, then Paul figured out a better place for it— closer to the house, right in front of the sliding-glass doors.

When the crane driver revved the engine, Eli, Paul, and Kate stood across the street and watched the giant bell lift slowly into the air. The clapper came loose from its binding and clanged against the sides of the bell as it moved above the garage and over the house to where the second driver—with Renee at his side—was positioned to steady the bell as it dropped into place.

As the bell's final tones were still ringing in their ears, they breathed a collective sigh of relief. But before the sigh had left their lips, Renee raced around the side of the house. "It's not where I wanted it," she shouted to Eli. "Don't pay these men until it's right."

"Lady, it's the only place it'll fit," the second driver said, shaking his head. He glanced at the crane driver, rolled his eyes, and shrugged.

Kate followed Renee around the outside of the house. There, in all its muddy, glorious beauty sat the bell. The morning sun was shining on it through the maple leaves, giving it a dappled sheen.

Kate stopped in her tracks. So did Eli and Paul behind her. Even Renee stopped her ranting and gaped at the bell.

It was a thing of beauty.

Kate blinked the sting of tears from her eyes, and she noticed that Renee did the same. Then Renee checked her watch, and gathering Kisses into her arms, headed off to her nail appointment.

KATE WAS UP AT DAWN Wednesday morning. She lit a fire in the fireplace, put on the coffee, then settled into her rocker for her morning talk with God. Since the middle of the night, something had been bothering her, but she couldn't put her finger on what it was.

She prayed for those on her mental prayer list, for the circumstances of the fire and its aftermath; for Paul and his ministry; for all their children; for Jed, who was getting out of jail later in the morning; and for their new congregation, as many by name as she could remember. She thought going through her list might trigger something in her mind, but it didn't.

She stepped outside to pick up the newspaper and breathed in the clear, crisp air. All signs of Sunday's drizzle were gone. The sun was just coming up, its slant causing the wet maple leaves to sparkle and shimmer.

It would have been more enjoyable if it hadn't been for that bothersome pinch at the edge of her brain.

But something just wouldn't let go of her. So she decided it was time to bake cookies.

She got out the recipes for three batches: oatmeal, dried cherries, and almonds; brown-sugar coconut bars; and pumpkin-persimmon spice with pecans, a new recipe she was trying out for the festival. She tried to keep her mind on the ingredients, but as usual, when she was puzzling something and baking cookies at the same time, the puzzling side of her brain took over.

She was in the middle of beating eggs for the brown-sugar bar cookies, trying to remember whether she had stirred in four or five, when the troublesome thought succeeded in burrowing through.

She stepped back, astounded.

At the same time, Paul came around the corner to kiss her good morning.

"You look like you've seen a ghost."

"Something's been bothering me since I talked to Sybil Hudson, and I just figured out what it was."

"I thought you said she was very helpful."

"She was. But do you remember how I said she told me about the CEO having grown up someplace around here?"

"Yes."

"What if he still has family ties here, longtime friends of the family, or family members themselves, who are in cahoots with the people at WDR?"

He poured a cup of coffee and sat down at the kitchen table. "It's possible, certainly."

"The stolen lumber, the bulldozer being rolled off a cliff, the fire itself—all of it could have been done by someone connected to WDR." She sat down across from Paul, leaning forward in her earnestness. "If we could make that connection, our mystery might be solved. We'd have our arsonist."

"I thought he'd left WDR."

"Yes, and I'm reasonably certain he wasn't that kind of player anyway. But what if he'd remained in contact with old friends and relatives throughout the years? Maybe contacted them when he was thinking about having his company buy the old hotel. Then WDR got in touch with them and got them on their side. After he left, they were still key players here in town, maybe put on the company payroll."

"The only thing that doesn't make sense is why they wouldn't remain loyal to family, to Charles."

"Money and power corrupt. Maybe they were offered something they couldn't refuse."

"How do we find them?"

She smiled. "That's what's been bothering me since three this morning."

Paul took a sip of coffee, his eyes crinkling as he watched her over the rim of the mug. "And you've just figured it out."

"I have," she said. "We don't find them. We let them come to us."

PAUL LEFT AT A QUARTER TO EIGHT to have breakfast with Eli and Sam at the diner, and Kate left for the town hall soon after.

When she arrived, she climbed the steps to the town hall, tempted to hurry to get to Jed and find out what he remembered about the fire. A few minutes later, she pushed through the entrance, crossed the large room, and burst through the deputy's-division doors.

Skip looked up and grinned. "Hey, Missus Hanlon. You're right on time."

"Hey, yourself." She fell into a chair to catch her breath and rub her knee. "Where's Jed?"

"He's coming. Sheriff just went down to get him."

A half hour later, the paperwork was complete, and Jed Packer walked out of the town hall a free man. Kate was at his side.

They stood for a moment at the top of the town hall steps, and he squinted in the sunlight. "Thank you for all you did, Mrs. Hanlon. It feels good to be free, to maybe start over again."

They walked down the stairs. "Do you need a ride anywhere? Back to the boarding house?"

"Thank you, but no." He smiled down at her. "I feel the need to walk. I need to be outside."

"I understand. But Paul and I want you to know that if you need anything, please just call or stop by." She told him how to find the parsonage. "Day or night."

"Thank you."

She turned to head to her car, then stopped. "In the excitement of your release, I forgot to ask. What did you remember about the fire?"

"It's about the baseball cap. The logo. It wasn't an animal. It was a pirate—a skull-and-crossbones type. And there was lettering, but I don't know what it was. Maybe three for four capital letters."

"Like a company name, a school? Something like that?"

He shrugged. "Something like that."

She blinked. Where had she seen such a cap? It seemed more familiar than ever.

KATE WAS JUST PULLING another sheet of cookies from the oven when Paul came through the door. He wasted no time getting to the kitchen. He grabbed the carton of milk, a glass, and a handful of pumpkin-persimmon spice pecan cookies, then sat down at the kitchen table. His expression said that heaven couldn't be better than this.

Kate laughed and slipped into a chair next to him. "How did your meeting go?"

He sobered and put down his cookie. "We talked about the rebuilding process, of course—the latest with the insurance, what we can expect in the payout. After that, Sam and I were ready to go, but Eli seemed to want to talk about other things." He paused thoughtfully. "He surprised me by asking if he could join our men's Bible study. He even asked if I've ever done a study on King David." Paul frowned. "I asked why David, and he said that he thought he might relate to him, which I found interesting."

Kate nodded thoughtfully. "David was God's friend. God referred to him as that, even after David grieved his Creator's heart because of his actions."

"Maybe that's what he's longing for after his months away from God and from the church—to become God's friend again."

"Eli has more depth than what I thought when we first met him," Kate said. "And a tender heart."

"He did have some good news related to our lumber."

Kate stood to get another plateful of cookies. "Another shipment?"

"A few weeks from now. And this time, twice the original order. Eli was thrilled."

"That's wonderful."

"The great thing about it is that things should really be moving along by then. Eli plans to have the rest of the rubble removed and maybe even the foundation poured. We found out that the insurance payout will be enough to do that much."

Paul took a bite of an oatmeal cookie, studying her face. "Why are you looking like that?"

"Like what?"

"Like you're about ready to rocket out of your chair and spin into orbit." He squinted and leaned closer. "There's that look in your eye I've seen before. You've got something planned. And something tells me I'm not going to like it."

"That's why I don't plan to tell you until it's ready to go." She put her hand on his. "So please be patient."

"You told me this morning you're going to get the WDR folks to come to you."

She nodded.

"That's what this is all about, isn't it? The delivery." Concern was etched in the lines of his face. "You know I worry about you, Katie."

She smiled and patted his cheek as she stood. "I'll have a cadre of sleuths with me. The plan is to set a trap and stay out of harm's way. The way I see it, nothing can go wrong. We won't even be nearby when the thieves roll in to do their mischief."

He reached for her hand. "I don't think mischief is quite the word for it." He sighed. "I know you want to get to the bottom of this, but this is a dangerous game you're playing. Sybil Hudson warned you that these people can get nasty."

She squeezed his fingers gently. "I'll be careful. I promise."

LIVVY AND KATE MET at the diner. LuAnne spotted them from behind the counter, put the coffeepot on the burner, then headed for their booth.

"What's up, darlin's?" LuAnne asked as she slid into the booth next to Kate.

Renee was sitting two tables over with a group of ladies. A smattering of others sat at other booths and tables. Kate smiled at three women she recognized from her tea.

"So, what's going on," LuAnne said.

"I've got an idea I need help with. Our next shipment of lumber is being delivered three weeks from now. I want to be there when it comes. I'm hoping you two will come with me."

"What?" LuAnne's voice came out in a croak. "You want to do what?"

"Hold a vigil across from the church property," Kate said. "Stay there all night if necessary so we catch the thieves red-handed."

LuAnne let out a slow whistle. "Girlfriend, you've got some guts."

Livvy was chuckling. "I like the idea. I'm in. Once in a while being a librarian can be a little, well . . ."

"Boring?" LuAnne finished for her.

"Actually, I was going to say *tame*."

LuAnne removed the pencil from above her ear and tapped the table. "Whatever. Count me in too, Kate. What's your plan?"

"I figure we'll get there early, hide ourselves somehow, dress warm, then just wait for the thieves to come."

"What do we do when the bad guys get there?" LuAnne wanted to know. "I mean, Livvy here probably weighs a hundred pounds soaking wet. As for me, I've got some meat on my bones, but I don't think I could fight my way out of a paper bag." She laughed heartily. "And Kate, darlin', compared to me, you look like you'd blow away in a strong wind." She leaned back in the booth, still smiling. "I can just see the three of us whoppin' on those guys."

"I don't think we'll need to whop on them," Kate said. "I simply want to get a description of their truck and a license number."

"That wouldn't be any fun," LuAnne said. "I say we make a human chain in front of the lumber. They have to run over us to get to it."

They all laughed.

"Okay, let's get down to business," Kate said. "This is what we need to do."

For the next several minutes, the women discussed the place and time and ways to disguise their hiding place. LuAnne said they could hide behind a patch of trees across from the church property, and Livvy suggested they simply park a car and stay inside with the lights out.

They were just getting into the details when Renee materialized in front of their booth. Kate wondered if the woman had rabbit ears.

"I overheard you talking about your plans to catch the perps," she said. "I want in."

"It'll be very cold. I don't think—" Kate began, then she saw the look on Renee's face and stopped. "Are you sure you want to do this?"

"I told you about BOLO."

Kate grinned. "That you did."

"This is part of my job. I'll be there. You just tell me where and when."

When she had returned to her booth, LuAnne leaned forward. "Darlin', what in the world's a bolo?"

Kate laughed. "You don't even want to know."

Chapter Eighteen

At nine o'clock that night, Kate called Livvy.

One of the Jenner boys answered, then yelled for his mom. There was a scuffling in the background, a faint sound of music, and snatches of conversation and laughter interspersed with a smattering of guffaws only a teen of the male variety could make. Kate knew that firsthand. Memories flew into her heart, and she swallowed a sting at the top of her throat.

"Hi, Kate," Livvy said a few minutes later.

"Hey, Watson," Kate said. "I've got a job for you. I got so caught up in the vigil plans, I forgot to ask."

"What's that?"

Kate told her about the baseball cap with the pirate logo. "Does that sound like anything you've seen?"

"No, it doesn't," Livvy said. "But it might be a school logo. Maybe a high school. I'll do a search tomorrow and let you know if anything comes up."

"Thanks, Liv."

"Anytime, Sherlock."

Kate hesitated before saying good-bye. "I probably don't need to say this, but enjoy every minute your kids are home. Time passes too quickly. And before you know it, the ruckus turns to silence."

"I know what you mean, but some days I can't wait." She laughed. "I know it'll hit me when they're finally gone, but I can't help singing "Bye Bye, Birdie" from time to time in anticipation."

The decibel level rose in the background, and Livvy said she had to go.

Kate hung up the phone and thought about Andrew, Rebecca, and Melissa. It seemed like just yesterday that her home was filled with laughter, music, and teenage tempers.

"I miss our kids," she said to Paul a few minutes later.

He was in bed, reading, and looked up when she spoke. "I do too."

She sat down on the edge of the bed to brush her hair. "Life changes can be difficult."

"And you've had a lot recently."

She smiled. "And you haven't?"

He laughed lightly. "I didn't mean that I haven't. But the empty-nest syndrome is real, and so is homesickness when you've been uprooted from the only town you've ever known. So is coming into a new situation where you've got to work to be accepted, to make new friends. So is not having a career outside the home for the first time in years. I'd say on the scale of life changes, you're off the charts."

She laughed. "Actually, I was only thinking about the

empty nest, but now that you mention all the rest . . ." She paused. "I just talked to Livvy, heard her kids in the background, and suddenly missed ours more than I can say."

"You could call them."

She checked the clock. "It's too late. I'll call in the morning."

"I know this is hard for you, Kate."

"It's getting easier," she said, hoping to relieve his worries. "Every day, a little easier."

She crawled into bed, wishing it were true.

ON SATURDAY, Kate decided it would be a good time to take down the wood paneling in the living room. The idea had come to her as she was finishing her Bible reading. The psalm for the day was the twenty-third, which brought to mind the sheep on the slider, which brought to mind the redecorating she wanted to do before Christmas. Though she had to admit she was starting to like the little flock of sheep. If she ever did decide to replace the sliders with French doors, she would miss them.

By the time Paul left to meet Pastor Bobby of the First Baptist Church, Father Lucas of St. Lucy's, and Pastor Pete of Copper Creek Presbyterian for their coffee get-together, Kate had already finished one wall.

Kate climbed up and down the ladder with her crowbar in hand, surprised at how fast the process was going. Each piece of four-by-eight-foot paneling was too big to handle by herself, so she let it drop to the floor for Paul to help her take out to the garage later.

The bare walls were worse than she had expected. Big splotches of black mastic had been smeared here and there, apparently as an adhesive. It had crystallized over the years and now was as hard as obsidian. She had hoped to start painting the walls in the afternoon, but the mastic would need sanding down first.

What she thought was a one- or two-day job was turning into something that would take a week to complete, probably with Paul working alongside her.

She was at the top of the ladder when the phone rang. For an instant she remained poised, midair, before deciding to run for the phone.

She got to the kitchen by the fourth ring and snatched up the receiver before it went to the answering machine.

"Kate?" said the voice.

She frowned, trying to place it.

"I was wondering if you could babysit today. Plus, I have some things I need to talk to you about."

Renee. She looked around in dismay. The little dog could get hurt with all the splintered wood and exposed nails.

"I need a massage," Renee said. "And little snookims can't go, bless his heart."

"I've got quite a mess around here," Kate said. "I'm taking down the paneling and . . ."

"Oh, that's quite all right," Renee said. "Kisses won't mind at all."

Kate sighed. "Okay. Bring him by."

Renee rang the doorbell five minutes later, Kisses in her arms. Renee was dressed in her usual designer warm-up suit and gold lamé tennis shoes. Not a bleached-blond hair was out of place.

At first glance, she looked the picture of health, but

beneath the makeup—heavy foundation and bright blush—
she looked tired. And no amount of concealer could hide the
dark circles under her eyes.

"Would you like to come in for a few minutes?"

"Well, yes, I was expecting to."

"How about some tea? I just bought some fresh loose-leaf
Earl Grey. Imported from England."

Renee put Kisses down. "Oh, I never drink Earl Grey
loose. It leaves sediment in the cup. I must use a tea bag.
Silk, if possible. And—"

"Three lumps of natural sugar. I remember. And
half-and-half."

Without waiting for an invitation, Renee barged into the
living room. "Oh dear. I see what you mean. You are in a bit
of a mess."

Kate went into the kitchen to put the teakettle on. She
fished around in the cupboard until she found the familiar
red and yellow box of tea bags, pulled one out, and dropped
it into a cup.

By the time the teakettle whistled, Renee had marched
into the kitchen and taken a place at the table. Kate poured
them each a cup of tea and set them on the table with the
sugar bowl.

Renee stirred in her three lumps. "I have some ideas for
the vigil and thought you should know about them."

"As I mentioned before, it's going to be a long, cold night.
And possibly dangerous."

Renee pulled a pink calendar book from her handbag,
flipped the pages to the current date, then pulled out a

matching pen. "We'll need food," she said. "Something warm, like soup in thermoses. I'll be in charge of that."

Kate nodded, smiling. "That would be very nice."

"And sandwiches. Can you make those?"

"I'd be happy to."

"I'll contact the others about what they can bring."

Alarmed, Kate sat forward. "What others?"

"I have a list of phone numbers. People who will be glad to help us out. Safety in numbers, I always say."

"Have you called anyone?"

She smiled. "I thought we would divide the list so one person doesn't have to do it all."

It was sounding more like a church picnic than a vigil.

"Renee, this is dangerous, too dangerous to invite anyone else. We're going to do this alone." She paused, sorry for the disappointment on Renee's face. "The other thing is that we don't want the thieves to know what we're doing."

Renee nodded. "I just thought we'd maybe need some backup when we confront the perps."

"We're not going to confront them—just find out who they are so we can call the authorities."

She brightened. "I happen to know I'm the only one with a cell phone. You need me! In fact, you can't do this without me." Her tone was triumphant. "And I'll bring my camera. We'll catch them red-handed."

"It's got a flash?"

She nodded.

"Then we can't use it."

Renee seemed to study the situation for a moment. She

took a sip of tea, shuddered, and said, "I think we're good enough friends that I can tell you this is the worst cup of tea I've ever had."

PAUL CAME IN THE DOOR just as Kate pulled off another sheet of paneling. Kisses woke from where he was sleeping by the fireplace and growled as Paul walked into the room.

He grinned. "I see we're babysitting little umpkins again."

Kate climbed back down the ladder. "It's my destiny. How was the coffee hour?"

"The guys are great. We discussed everything from politics to theology, the NFL to deep-sea fishing." He chuckled. "We certainly don't agree on everything, but our discussion was spirited and accepting of the other points of view."

They went into the kitchen and sat down at the table. "You won't believe what they've got planned for the pumpkin festival. They've asked their congregations to donate items or services for our auction."

"Oh, Paul. That's wonderful."

"There's more. They wanted to give their congregations examples of creative thinking.

"Father Lucas, the Episcopalian priest, is a private pilot and has his own plane. He's donating free plane rides for the auction, as many as we want. And Pastor Pete, the Presbyterian minister, says he knows where all the best fishing holes are in the area. People have been after him for years to reveal where they are. His auction contribution is to sell his top-ten secret spots. Not only that, he's also donating his time as a guide for the winner.

"And listen to this one: Pastor Bobby of the Baptist church told us his wife writes and illustrates children's picture books. She's working on her second book right now. She came up with a brilliant idea—auctioning off the chance to pick a pet, and its name, as a sidekick for her main character. Dog, cat, pot-bellied pig, or hamster—he said it doesn't matter. She'll work it into the story."

"I'm overwhelmed," Kate said. "Not just their creativity, which is incredible. But love in action . . ."

"Preach Christ, and if you must, use words," he quoted. He hesitated for a moment as if mulling something over, then he said, "There's still more."

"I can't imagine it getting any better than this."

"I made a decision as I was driving home."

"It sounds momentous."

"It is. I've decided to donate the Lexus to the auction."

Kate's eyes filled with tears, and she reached for his hand.

Chapter Nineteen

At the same time Kate began painting the living room, work began in earnest on the church property. Eli had arranged for six heavy-duty trucks to haul away debris, and an earthmover to come in once the ground was cleared to level the soil. Two weeks later, the foundation was poured, and framing was ready to begin.

Kate was pleased with the transformation of the room. She had painted the newly smooth walls a soft ivory, and new drapes hung over the huge sliders. Paul had removed the fluorescent lighting and acoustic pebbling on the ceiling, and she had added torch floor lamps for soft, indirect lighting. She also put ivory and light tan slip covers on the sofa, love seat, and overstuffed chairs. A scattering of throw pillows in primary hues added a splash of color.

She arranged the sitting area around the fireplace, separate from the rest of the large room, which she needed to keep clear of furniture for Sunday services. The spinet piano and Paul's bookcases lined the walls, though she had left plenty of space for artwork.

Above the piano, she hung a framed calligraphy print of the prayer of Saint Francis of Assisi—"Lord, make me an instrument of thy peace . . ." Three other large framed prints were of a Southwest design and had hung in their San Antonio home. They were paintings of two missions in California—the Carmel and the San Juan Capistrano—and one in New Mexico.

The moss green shag carpet still covered the floor. She and Paul had paid for the new paint and drapes out of their own pocket, but they didn't feel now was the time to go to any added expense for the church, or themselves. Too many other needs took precedence.

Kate's favorite new addition, though, was the church bell that graced the tiny backyard. Though Paul and Kate had scrubbed and polished the bell, the damage from the fire was still evident. But that didn't seem to matter when the morning sun hit it and turned it back into the beautiful bronze bell it once was.

THE MORNING THE LUMBER DELIVERY was due to arrive dawned gray and dreary with the promise of coming rain. Kate was sitting at the kitchen table reading the morning *Chronicle*. She groaned as she read the weather report. "Oh no, not today." She pictured the vigil in pouring rain and sighed.

The phone rang, interrupting her thoughts. It was LuAnne asking if Kate had seen the weather report. The next call was from Livvy asking the same thing. The third call was from Lester Philpott, a member of Faith Briar whom Kate had met once before.

"I understand you do pet sitting," he said.

For a moment, Kate was too stunned to answer.

"*Um* . . . Renee Lambert gave me your name and number."

"I do watch her Chihuahua from time to time . . ."

"You see, this is sort of an emergency. My mother Enid—I don't think you've met her—has this cat named Ruffles. Ruffles doesn't get along with Maximillian, the rottweiler me and my brother LeRoy have. In fact, he attacks Maximillian every chance he gets."

"You and LeRoy live with your mother?" She blurted out before she could stop herself.

"Oh yes." He chuckled. "For some reason we just never left home."

One thing worse than an empty nest would be two middle-aged chicks still in it, Kate thought. *Talk about singing "Bye Bye, Birdie" . . .*

"Anyway," Lester went on, "we had to take Mother to the hospital last night. Emergency gall-bladder surgery. Maximillian was with us, but the minute we opened the door, Ruffles attacked him. You see, Mother is the referee. She's the only one Ruffles will mind. Maximillian might be ten times bigger, but this cat is a bully."

"How's your mother?"

"I spoke with the doctor on the phone a few minutes ago. She's resting well. But she'll be in the hospital at least three days."

Kate took a deep breath. "Then, of course, bring Ruffles over. I'll take care of him."

Lester arrived with a yowling cat in a carrier a half hour later. He returned to the car and came back with a litter box and a sack of sensitive-stomach cat food.

"I can't thank you enough," he said, then trotted back down the sidewalk.

Kate came back in the house to find the big long-haired tabby sitting on the kitchen counter eyeing the big Crock-Pot of chicken soup she had made for dinner. "Don't even think about it!" She wagged her finger at him.

The gleam in his big green eyes said he was indeed thinking about it, and what's more, he would politely wait until her back was turned to do a taste test.

He took his time getting off the counter, then turned his back to Kate and groomed his whiskers.

At 5:30 that night, Livvy swung by to pick up Kate in the Jenner SUV. LuAnne was already with her, grinning as if this was the grandest outing ever.

Five minutes later, Renee Lambert had plopped into the backseat, and they were heading toward a patch of trees across from the church property.

The sun had set, and the coming twilight would help their cover. Livvy parked behind a dense thicket of trees, and the four women clambered out of the car. It was already cold, and Kate shivered, holding her down parka close.

The rain never materialized, but in its place a bone-chilling wind had kicked up.

LuAnne blew on her hands and stomped her feet. "Whoa, baby. It's chilly out here."

"Are you sure we can't have a campfire?" Renee wanted to know.

"I'm sure," Kate said, though the idea appealed to her. She pulled her gloves out of her parka pocket and yanked them over her fingers, already stiff with cold.

Livvy pulled folding lawn chairs out of the back of the SUV. Each of the women took one, lined it up with the others on one side of the trees, and sat down. They could clearly see the new pile of lumber, stacked higher than before. They each had binoculars strung around their necks. Kisses was curled in Renee's lap, snoring like a chain saw, which worried Kate. She could have kicked herself for not telling Renee to leave him home.

"Once it gets dark, we won't be able to see a thing," LuAnne whispered.

"I hope they leave the headlights on when they pick up the lumber," Livvy said.

"We'll need to move behind the trees if they do," Kate said. "If they back the truck in, the headlights will beam right where we're sitting."

"I bet that would surprise 'em," LuAnne said. "Can you imagine, darlin's, thinkin' you're all alone, then lookin' across the street where four women with binoculars are sittin' there starin' back at you?" She laughed. "Don't you love it?"

An hour later, the hum of a vehicle caught their attention. The chatting stopped as headlights approached, but the car drove on without stopping. "You don't suppose we're too obvious, do you?" LuAnne wanted to know a half hour later. "Maybe they've somehow spotted us."

"I'm hungry," Renee said. "Let's get out the soup."

Out came the sandwiches and soup—served in double-thick paper cups—coffee, tea, and hot cider. Kate opened a container of chocolate-chip cookies and passed them around.

They talked about the pumpkin festival, sharing recipes and ideas for crafts to sell. Renee told them about a secret pumpkin-pie recipe that had been in her family for decades. "I'm sure I'll win," she said, and no one argued. Renee might miss the mark on her social skills, but no one could argue that she wasn't one of the best cooks in town.

It was almost midnight when the low rumble of a big truck slowly approached. The group fell silent.

Kate's heart missed a beat or two, and she held her breath.

The truck stopped in front of the church property, and two men crawled out of the cab. They had high-beam flashlights and shone them around as they walked toward the lumber. After a few minutes, the driver got back in the truck and swung around to back into the driveway.

Briefly the monster headlights swung across the row of vigilantes. There was a collective gasp.

"Oh no!" LuAnne breathed.

But the driver obviously didn't notice he was being watched. He jumped out of the cab again and opened the back of the truck with a clatter and a bang.

"I want to go get them now," LuAnne said. "I'm steamed. They're takin' what doesn't belong to them."

Renee stood up and handed kisses to Kate. "I'm ready. I'll go with you."

"No, please," Kate said. "They've got to be caught with the lumber in the truck. Do you have your cell phone ready, Renee?"

"Sure do." Renee nodded, then reached into her purse for the portable phone. She was the only one of the four who owned one, and they planned to call the police with it as soon as the truck was loaded. "Oh no." Renee shook her head and pushed a few buttons on the phone.

"What's wrong?" Livvy asked.

"It's dead," Renee sighed. "I always forget to charge it."

Kate began a silent count to ten.

"What are we going to do without a phone?" LuAnne asked. "How are we going to stop them?"

Kate reached eight and a half, decided she was calm enough to speak, and said, "We may not be able to get the cops to catch them red-handed, but maybe we can pick up a clue about where they're headed."

"*Hmmph*," Renee said.

An hour crawled by. Then another half hour. The men weren't in any hurry. They laughed and joked while they worked, stopped every few minutes for a cigarette or a beer, then went back to their loading.

Kate was shivering now, and her feet were numb. A light mist had started to fall. Renee sneezed, which made Kate worry about her health. What if it started to rain? They would have no choice but to leave, and their cover would be blown.

At one thirty, Renee stood up and said she'd had enough; she wanted to go home.

The others looked at each other in dismay. They were so close. Only a few boards were scattered on the ground.

"Furthermore," she said. "I intend to walk over there and give them a piece of my mind."

"The truck's almost loaded," Livvy said. "Can't you wait just a little while longer? We'll get the information we need and go home."

"No. I've made up my mind. These perps are about to get a free trip to the slammer. They're about to get popped." She paused, wagging her finger at the others. "And don't try to stop me. I've got a plan, but it'll only work if the perps think I'm alone. Give me five minutes. If I need you, I'll holler."

She handed the Chihuahua to Kate again and—before the others could utter a cautionary word—she put her shoulders back and took off for the building site, waving her flashlight at the ground as she picked her way around shrubs and clumps of autumn-dry grass.

"Popped?" LuAnne whispered.

"And sent to the hoosegow," Livvy said, grinning.

The three gave each other worried looks and stood, their attention riveted to the building site.

"Excuse me, sirs?" They heard Renee's voice carry from across the street. "Helloooo?"

Some sharp expletives rose from behind the truck, then the men came around from where they had been working.

"What th—" the driver said. "Who're you?"

"My car broke down a ways down the road. I'm wondering if you all could give me a ride. Looks like you're about through here. Where are you headed?"

"Look, little lady," the second man said, "we're not in the taxicab business, so I suggest you git on down the road you came from."

The driver added. "We're on a job, otherwise we'd try to do something. We'll call the sheriff once we're outta here, though. Tell him about you being stranded and all."

"Yeah, right. We'll do just that."

"Which way are you going?" Renee said. "Just so I know if it's out of your way or not. What would it hurt? My car's not very far . . ."

"It is out of our way," the driver said. "You'll have to make do on your own."

"And we ain't callin' no sheriff," the second man said. "I'm in charge, and I'm saying we ain't callin' no cops."

Kate watched Renee bravely continue to try to wheedle information out of the men. The woman was shivering in the cold; Kate could see it even from a distance.

She couldn't stand it any longer. LuAnne and Livvy obviously felt the same way. They all stood at once and started walking across the road, flashlights in hand.

The men looked up, fear in their eyes, faces pale, mouths gaping. Kate realized with a nervous giggle, which she quickly swallowed, that the truckers couldn't see who was behind the beams of light. The vigilantes of Copper Mill probably looked threatening.

The men scrambled into the truck cab, revved the engine, scraped the gears, and pulled out of the church parking lot.

Everyone started talking at once as they gathered around Renee to see if she was okay. She shrugged off the attention, and with a sniff, pulled her pink-covered planner out of her coat pocket. She fished around for her pen, then wrote something on the page under the day's date.

She held it up for everyone to see. Three flashlight beams hit the pad at once, turning it, appropriately, a lustrous white.

"The license plate number, ladies. I think we got our perps. And believe you me, they're not going to beat this rap."

Chapter Twenty

Kate's routine changed the minute Ruffles pranced through their house, tail swishing like a flag. Every time Kate sat down, the cat hopped onto her lap, curled three times before getting comfortable, purred for a few minutes, then slept. She suspected the cat weighed at least twenty pounds, though he looked like he could be closer to thirty because of his thick, long hair.

When the phone rang at eight o'clock the morning after the vigil, Kate was sitting by the fire, thinking over the happenings of the night before. She made a flying attempt to get to the kitchen before the call clicked over to the answering machine. Ruffles catapulted across the room with an indignant yowl as Kate ran to the kitchen.

She grabbed the phone.

"Missus Hanlon?"

She knew his voice by now. "Hello, Skip. Did you find anything out?"

"We surely did. Ran a database search and found out who they are. Also found the lumber. The sheriff said you all did fine work."

"But you didn't catch the men?" Kate fell into a chair at the kitchen table.

"Nah. They unhooked the cab from the trailer and skedaddled."

"Can we connect them to the fire?"

"Too early to tell, but the prospects look good." He paused. "You were right—what you said about them being relatives of that CEO, the one that started that whole thing with the hotel."

"How'd you find that out?" Ruffles jumped into her lap, curled, and purred. She rubbed his ears, making fur fly. Then she sneezed, which scared the cat. He jumped off her lap as if he'd been shot and raced into the living room.

"Are you all right?" Skip wanted to know.

She laughed. "I'm babysitting Enid Philpott's cat and just scared the wits out of the big guy."

"Ruffles? I know that cat."

It was one thing for everyone in town to know each other, but they knew everyone's pets too? "You do?"

"I had to get him off Enid's roof last summer. Ruffles got out—you do know, don't you, that he's an indoor cat?"

"Yes, I do."

"I just wanted to make sure. Anyway, someone left the door open. Enid thinks it was LeRoy, who can be absent-minded at times. They didn't even know he was missing until the middle of the night when they heard his cry coming through the fireplace."

"He got stuck in the chimney?"

"Oh no. He was just looking over the top and felt like

meowing, I guess. The funny thing was, Enid and her boys looked all over the house because the sound didn't seem to be coming from anyplace in particular.

"Enid said later she thought God was calling out to her in the middle of the night. Nearly scared her to death."

"She thought God might sound like a cat?"

"Oh no. She knew better than that. She'd gone to bed exhausted and didn't say her prayers. She was worried he was upset with her.

"To make a long story even longer . . ."—he chuckled at his own joke—"I came into the house to search for Ruffles and found him right off the bat."

"How'd you do it?"

"Rattled his bag of cat food. That'll bring any cat running in no time. If he ever gets away from you, that's all you've got to do."

"I'll remember that."

"I rattled it in every room. And if you can believe it, when I rattled it by the fireplace, he yowled something fierce. We knew right away where to find him. There was only one thing wrong with my plan."

"He came down the chimney?"

"Yep, slick as a whistle and twice as fast. Though he got stuck partway down."

"How'd you get him out?"

"I didn't. We had to call the fire department. And when Ruffles finally got out, he was no longer a tabby. He was as black as midnight. And his voice was so hoarse, he couldn't meow for a week. Enid was fit to be tied." Skip let out a long sigh. "That was another of those reasons the sheriff put me on a desk job. The first one was when I arrested Renee Lambert for pickpocketing."

"I heard about that."

"I think I'm destined to sit behind a desk."

"You're a good deputy, Skip. Don't let anyone tell you otherwise."

"Thanks," he said.

"Now, back to how you connected the thugs to the CEO."

"That part was easy. The truck is registered to someone with the same last name, though without the triple toothpicks."

"The what? Oh yes, Charles Brandsmyth III."

"This one's just Clarence Brandsmyth."

"Thanks for letting me know," Kate said. "But I still can't rest easy." She hesitated, then added, "You're not going to stop looking for them, are you?"

"Not on your life, Missus Hanlon. We'll find 'em in no time. Then you can rest easy."

Kate didn't put the receiver back in its cradle but held it in her hand, staring at it, weighing whether to call Renee to see how she was after spending the night out in the drizzly cold. But the woman could be so prickly if people tried to show her they cared.

She finally punched in Renee's number. She let the phone ring ten times before disconnecting. She tried not to worry, but as she went about her morning chores, her thoughts kept going back to the woman.

An hour later, she tried again. Still no answer.

Again, she tried to dismiss it. Renee could be getting her nails done or her roots bleached, or having a massage.

At noon, Paul came home from a meeting with Eli. He had a spring in his step, and when he saw her in the kitchen, he pulled her into his arms and did a jig around the kitchen.

"Things must be going well," she said, grinning up at him as he twirled, then dipped her.

Laughing, they headed to the living room. "We're cookin' now," he said. "Eli's the wonder kid. He's found people all over the state in the construction industry who want to help us. He told them about the fire, the insurance fiasco, and our dire financial straits." He shook his head slowly. "In some cases, they're donating their materials or skills; in others, they're giving us a discount. That young man has worked tirelessly. Today, for the first time, I can see that we may actually get a church built."

"Which reminds me. Skip called and said they found the lumber."

He frowned. "What about the two men?"

"Not yet." She told him about the family connection to the former CEO. "At least we know their identities," she said.

She didn't tell him how nervous she was driving around town. Every time she drove out of the garage, she checked the street to make sure no one was waiting.

She checked her rearview mirror constantly to see if someone was tailing her. Every stop at the grocery store, every trip to visit Livvy or LuAnne, she was hypervigilant. She had hoped it would all be over after last night. Apparently, it wasn't.

Paul reached for her hand. "It was still a great success. Now we know their identities. They may be the ones who started the fire on behalf of WDR—and lead us to whoever was behind the plan." He smiled. "Thanks to you, we're halfway there."

"And Renee. I'll never forget how she just marched right up to the thugs and demanded they give her a ride."

Ruffles wandered around the corner, sat down by the fireplace, licked his paw, then fixed a green-eyed stare on Paul.

"I ran into Bobby Evans this morning. Enid Philpott is a member of his church."

"That's odd. Her sons come to Faith Briar."

Paul nodded. "Bobby said Enid isn't doing well. She'll need to stay in the hospital for a few more days."

"I'm sorry."

"I am too." He hesitated, then added, "Ruffles may be here for some time."

Ruffles had now flipped over on his back with his eyes closed. Kate stood and ruffled his tummy, then went in to call Renee again.

Still no answer.

"I'm going to run over to Renee's with some soup," she told Paul, "and make sure she's okay."

TWENTY MINUTES LATER, she was driving down Smoky Mountain Road. There had been no cars on her street when she pulled out of the garage, but now, suddenly, a dark SUV was behind her.

She turned right onto Ashland and checked her mirror.

The SUV was still there. The windshield was tinted, and she couldn't see any faces, which made her shiver.

She told her heart to quit hammering her ribs, then felt foolish when she turned onto Renee's street and the SUV kept going straight.

Her knees were weak when she climbed out of the Honda, and her fingers ached from clutching the steering wheel so hard.

Kate had to laugh at herself as she reached for the container of chicken soup. She was letting her imagination work overtime.

She rang Renee's doorbell. There was no sound inside, which worried her. She rang it again, and this time she heard barking.

Then Kisses scritch-scratched on the back of the door as if trying to get out.

Kate tried the elegant brass handle, but it was locked. She rang the doorbell again, then lifted her hand to knock.

The door slowly opened, and Renee stood in front of her. She wore slim black slacks, a leopard-skin-print silk blouse, and high heels with jeweled buckles. Her makeup and hair were perfect, but there was something about her expression that squeezed Kate's heart.

"Oh," Kate said. "I've been phoning, and just now when you didn't come to the door, I thought . . . well, I got worried."

"You don't need to worry about me," Renee said.

"I brought you some soup."

Her sigh came out in a "*hmmph*," but she took the container anyway and headed to the kitchen. Kate followed.

She put the soup container on the gleaming black-granite counter. A recipe box sat to one side, and a small note card with a handwritten recipe was propped up against it. Renee quickly flipped the card over. Then she turned back to Kate. "Life might be taking an unexpected turn right now, but let me tell you, I don't need your help or pity or anything else." She set her mouth in a straight line and turned away.

Kate thought she saw Renee's chin quiver. "What is it, Renee? Are you ill? Is that what all your appointments have been about?"

"Ha, now that's a stretch." Renee waved her away. "Now, if you'll excuse me. I'm expecting a . . . ah . . . guest." She hurried Kate toward the front door, but as Kate stepped through the entry hall, she glanced into the room where she'd had coffee with Renee the previous month.

Most of the furniture had been moved out, and in its place was a hospital bed. The pillow end was propped up so that it faced the window and the garden outside, bright with mums and chrysanthemums.

Kate stopped midstep and took in the room. "You have friends. There are people at Faith Briar who care about you. Whatever it is, let us help."

Renee stared at her, eyed the bed, then looked back to Kate. "Friends?" Her voice was unexpectedly soft. She walked closer to the bed and laid one hand across the mattress. Even from a few feet away, Kate noticed the sheets smelled fresh, and the blankets looked soft and new. A teddy bear was propped up against the pillow. Fresh-cut flowers cascaded from a vase on a bedside lamp table.

Renee noticed Kate's confused look. "This is for my best

friend. Probably the only true friend I've ever had." She smiled. She walked to the window and looked out. "She'll be here any minute."

Kate took a deep breath, wanting to leave but feeling called to stay. "I brought enough soup for you both tonight. I would have brought more, enough for tomorrow night if I had known . . ."

Renee stared at her, blinked rapidly as if something was in her eye, then said, "Thank you."

An ambulance pulled to the curb outside Renee's house. She drew back the curtain and said, "She's here."

Kate followed her to the front door and stood to one side as two uniformed men carried a small bundle of an elderly woman with white hair into the house on a mobile hospital cot. They turned into the room with the bed.

After the men left, Renee went into the room. Kate stepped to the doorway to say good-bye, but Renee surprised her by signaling her in. "There's someone I want you to meet," she said to Kate.

Kate moved to the side of the bed and looked down. She almost gasped. It could have been Renee herself in that bed, only this woman was twenty-some years older. The woman had the same perfect makeup and coiffed hair, which Kate suspected was a wig, and wore an animal-print silky nightgown.

"Kate, this is my mother, Caroline Beauregard Johnston, granddaughter of the greatest Civil War hero in Tennessee, J. P. Beauregard . . . and my best friend," Renee said. "Mama, meet Mrs. Hanlon, the new minister's wife I told you about."

"Did you ask her yet?" The old woman fixed a piercing gaze on her daughter.

Renee let out a sarcastic *"hmmph."* "Just give me a chance, Mama. What do you think this is, a five-star hotel with a concierge?"

"You know what I told you, Missy. I cannot abide little yipping dogs. We cannot stay in the same house. If need be, I'll hitchhike back to Green Acres where I should've stayed in the first place." She continued staring hard at Renee.

Kate broke in. "The question please?" Though she had a good inkling of what it was. All she could think of was how Ruffles might eat little umpkins for a midnight snack.

"I was planning to ask if you could take Kisses for a few days."

"Few days!" Mama almost shouted. "I'm not going to the big beyond that fast, Missy. All I've got is a broken hip, not terminal cancer."

"What will you do without your little dog?" Kate asked Renee.

"I can visit."

"Hmmph" rose from the bed. "Little umpkins this, little umpkins that."

"I'll be happy to take care of him for you," Kate said. "Really."

"My mother's allergic . . ."

There was a choking cough behind them. "No, I just don't like little yipping Chihuahuas."

"Now, you listen up," Renee said. "If I say you're allergic, you're allergic. I still have my marbles. I remember what the doctor said on my last visit. You're asthmatic."

"Maybe I'd better go," Kate said, sidling toward the door. "If you'll get Kisses' things . . ."

Renee's eyes brimmed with tears as she held the dog close.

"Come visit anytime," Kate said when they were outside.

She put Kisses on the ground and handed the leash to Kate. "Some things in life just can't be helped."

She straightened her shoulders, glanced one more time at Kisses, then with a sigh, returned to the house. Now Kate understood the sad expression she had seen in Renee's eyes earlier.

"Anytime," Kate called after her. She was surprised that she meant it.

Chapter Twenty-One

It was a rainy and cold Friday evening when Kate flipped on the porch light, locked the house, and headed to the garage. Paulwas in Chattanooga, visiting Nehemiah, and wasn't expected home until later.

The forecast called for a light snow by morning. She worried about Paul, though he promised to stay with Nehemiah if the weather worsened.

She backed out of the garage with the wipers swishing across the windshield. The ping of ice pellets on the glass told her the rain was already turning to sleet. She wore a heavy coat, and the car's heater was on high, but she was still shivering.

Ten minutes later, she parked at the Country Diner, grabbed her handbag, eased herself out of the car, and opened her umbrella.

The lights in the diner were inviting, and she hurried to the front door, being careful of the slick pavement.

She stepped inside, waved to a couple of women who had come to her tea, then spotted Livvy waiting at what was becoming their favorite booth. LuAnne was serving two men at a separate booth on the opposite side.

"Hey, Mrs. Hanlon!" a voice called from behind the counter. She looked up to see Jed grinning at her.

She toodled her fingers to Livvy, then walked over to say hello to him.

"I've got a new job. Short-order cook on the late shift. I can fry up some mean hamburgers and fries."

"Then that's what I'll have tonight."

Jed's transformation was astounding. His hair was trimmed and neat, he wore new clothes, and there was a confident bounce to his step. "You look great," she said.

"I'm feelin' good," he said. "It's been a long time coming." As she turned to walk away, he added, "And you were right, Mrs. Hanlon."

"*Hmm*," she said, though with a smile. She had almost reached the booth where Livvy waited when she figured out what he was talking about.

She turned again. Jed was still watching her, his eyes bright.

She had told him about God's forgiveness, mercy, and grace, and he was telling her he now understood.

She met his eyes across the room and nodded. Only then did he return to the short-order grill.

IT WAS DINNERTIME, and the diner was filling fast with customers, so LuAnne could only sit with Livvy and Kate for a few minutes at a time. She popped up and down, waiting on people as they came in, then returning.

"Two things I've gotta tell you first, girlfriends," she said, her cheeks pink. "You see who's over in that corner. No, don't look right at him, if you know what I mean. Just sort of glance sideways."

"It's Lester Philpott," Livvy said.

LuAnne leaned in, whispering. "Check out the booth in the opposite corner from where Lester is sitting."

"Okay, I'm looking," Livvy said.

"So am I," Kate said as she turned. But LuAnne was standing in the way, and Kate couldn't see anything. "What is it?" Kate whispered. "Who's there?"

"It's the same guys who were in here a few weeks ago. The guys from WDR." LuAnne shook her head. "You'd think they'd be too ashamed to raise their heads after we caught their thugs in action."

"There's no proof the thugs are connected to them," Kate said. "And until they're found, we can't connect them to the fire. It's the missing piece of the puzzle."

"They just upped and disappeared." LuAnne pulled a heavy pad out of her pocket and handed it to Kate. "You two go over my list . . . See if I've forgotten anything and write it down. Maybe we can meet again next week—see if we're gettin' our quail in a clutch."

"Covey, I think you mean," Livvy said, grinning.

"Well, then, quail in a covey," LuAnne amended. "Now, gettin' down to real business—what can I get you two to eat?"

They ordered, and while they waited, Livvy and Kate discussed the details of the festival. LuAnne had met with the mayor and city council, and they had agreed to block off three blocks of Main Street for the festival.

Booths selling everything from homemade pumpkin fudge to painted saws would line the street and spill into the park next to Main Street. One side of the park would be set up for the Little Miss Pumpkin and Little Mister Pumpkin contests.

"I asked Eli to see if he can find bleachers somewhere," LuAnne said when she brought their food. "Also make a podium for us."

"We'll need a sound system," Kate said.

Livvy volunteered Danny. "I'm sure he can get something from the high school." She looked up from taking notes. "I contacted the three churches in town, and they've all opened their kitchens to us.

"There's something else." Livvy grinned. "We've got a marching band to lead the pumpkin parade. We tried to get East Tennessee State, but they couldn't do it. Danny talked to the bandleader at his school, and they've agreed to open our festivities!"

LuAnne and Kate cheered. "This is really coming together," Kate said.

"Darlin's, the buzz is incredible," LuAnne said. "All day long I hear folks chattin' about what they're makin' or what they're plannin' to buy or sell or both. The auction is the talk of the town, and, Kate, your hubby has become quite the topic of conversation."

"Because of the car?"

"You got it, darlin'. Everybody in town is plannin' to bid on it."

Someone asked for a refill, so LuAnne trotted across the

diner to the counter and grabbed the coffeepot to make her rounds.

"They left," LuAnne said when she returned. "The men from WDR. If I didn't have to work, I'd follow them. Maybe they'd lead us to Clarence whatshisname."

"Brandsmyth," Kate said.

"They were in a big SUV. Fancy thing. One of those Hummers, I think. Or maybe it was a Cadillac." LuAnne squinted at Kate. "Darlin', you look a little peaked. Are you all right?"

"It's just that a couple of times recently, I had a strange feeling I was being followed. There was a big SUV behind me, but I couldn't tell you what kind it was." Kate shook her head. "It's just me being paranoid. I'm beginning to see bogeymen behind every tree."

Kate checked her watch, pulled out a bill to pay for her meal, then stood to leave. "Paul's in Chattanooga and said he'd call about now to tell me if he's going to brave the weather. I need to be home for the call."

"You be careful now, darlin'," LuAnne said, looking worried.

Livvy nodded. "How about if I follow you in my car? Make sure you get there okay."

"Oh goodness, no," Kate said. "I'll be fine. I'm only a few blocks from home."

The women said their good-byes, and Kate hurried to her car, holding up the umbrella. The rain was turning to sleet in earnest now. The wipers swished in rhythm as she pulled out of the parking lot, but the icy rain made it difficult for them to clear the windows.

She had a white-knuckle grip on the steering wheel all the way home, feeling the tires slide each time she made a turn. She let out a pent-up breath of relief once she pulled into the garage. She hoped Paul wouldn't attempt coming home from Chattanooga in this, especially in the sporty Lexus, which had never been a good snow or ice car.

The sleet hit her umbrella as she walked to the front door.

The porch light was out, which puzzled her. She dismissed it, thinking the bulb had burned out. She found the lock and placed her key into the hole, turned it until it clicked, then pushed open the door.

Someone had been in the house. She didn't know how she knew it; she just did.

Heart pounding, she flipped on the entry light and checked the living room. Ruffles, who was asleep by the fireplace, looked up and blinked.

Now Kisses started scratching at the spare bedroom door, where Kate had left him for protection from Ruffles. The two were still getting used to each other, though there hadn't been any major incidents yet.

Maybe it was her imagination that someone had been here in her absence. After all, she wasn't used to having indoor pets. Her kids had had a desert tortoise for a pet when they were little, but that was about the extent of it.

While her umbrella was still up, she retrieved the Chihuahua and took him out to the maple tree, holding the umbrella over him. The little dog did his business, shivering the whole time, then Kate took him back into the house where Ruffles sat by the door, looking hungry and irritated.

She had just fed Kisses when the phone rang. She was closer to the bedroom phone, so she picked it up there.

"Mrs. Hanlon?" The sound was garbled as if the caller was on a cell phone.

"Yes."

Again the line was garbled and filled with static. She made out the words "your husband...injured...asked to call you...needs help. Please come..." And finally, "Rural Route 2."

There was more, but Kate couldn't make it out.

She ran to the kitchen to feed a now yowling and even more frantic Ruffles, rounded the corner by the fridge, and stopped dead in her tracks.

There on the kitchen table was a small black box, tied with a black ribbon. It hadn't been there when she left. And she knew Paul hadn't been home since she left.

Trembling, she walked over to it.

Someone *had* been in her house while she was gone.

She stared down at it for a moment, knowing she needed to get to Paul right away. But she was also curious to see what was inside.

Her heart pounded as she lifted the lid. Something was covered with black tissue paper, as if it was a gift. A ghoulish gift.

She frowned and pulled out the tissue. There, staring up at her was a stuffed toy Chihuahua. Its throat had been sliced, and its stuffing was falling out.

She stared at it, almost afraid to breathe. Her knees were as weak as a newborn deer's and threatened to fold beneath her.

The arsonist had been here, in her home, in this very room. He had left this as a warning.

First, the death threat. Now this.

She clutched the table to stop her hands from shaking, gulped a deep breath, and prayed she wouldn't throw up. She didn't have time.

Paul needed her.

Chapter Twenty-Two

K ate tossed a handful of dried cat food in Ruffles' dish, ran to her car, got in, slammed the door, and backed out of the driveway with a squeal of tires.

She raced through town, vaguely remembering where the cutoff was for Route 2. She slowed at several cross streets, straining to make out the signs in the dark, then finally found it about a mile east of Copper Mill.

She wound along the country road, through rolling hills. She had only one goal, and that was to get to Paul.

She was alone on the road. The rhythm of the wipers was oddly comforting, but as she climbed out of the valley, the rain began to pelt her windshield.

She knew the sound. It meant sleet, and she prayed it didn't also mean ice or snow at the higher elevations.

She was still dealing with that unsettling thought when headlights appeared behind her. Approaching fast.

At first she was glad to know she wasn't alone on the road, then the vehicle came up behind her. The height of the headlights told her this wasn't an ordinary car. It was much bigger. An oversized SUV or Hummer.

"Oh, Lord," she breathed. "Be with me. Help me."

The hulk of a vehicle came closer, almost touching her bumper. She increased her speed.

So did the hulk.

The narrow road was winding up a steep hill now, gaining elevation with each mile. Kate had to slow because of the curves and switchbacks. With each turn of the car, her headlights beamed through the now-falling snow into a dark abyss. On the opposite side, the road hugged the mountain.

There was no place to turn around, even if she could get past the SUV.

Her greatest hope was to get to the accident site soon, or at least to meet the emergency vehicles on their way to Copper Mill.

The snow was falling faster now, and though Paul always kept good tires on her Honda, she could feel them skid on the corners.

She slowed to regain control.

That's when the SUV hit her back bumper. She clutched the steering wheel with a death grip as the car careened wildly. She looked in her rearview mirror.

The occupants of the SUV were hidden in the darkness and snow, and by the tinted windows.

She clung to the steering wheel, bracing herself for the next nudge, and prayed they were just trying to frighten her, nothing more.

Then she remembered the accident in California.

Her heart hammered against her ribs, and she thought she might pass out. She wanted to get mad, which she thought might serve her better in a crisis. But she was too scared to muster up the smallest bit of anger.

The SUV lagged back, and she breathed a little easier. Then, horrified, she watched it speed toward her and hit her bumper with even greater force.

This time the Honda spun wildly out of control. No matter how she turned the wheel, it was as if the car had taken on a life of its own. She bounced against the side of the mountain, scraping against rocks, only to skid back across the highway, hit a guardrail, and bounce back again.

The car finally spun to a stop, crisscrossing the road.

All was quiet.

Kate prayed harder than she had ever prayed before. She didn't pray for herself but for Paul, who needed her. She wasn't going to make it to him.

She heard the SUV rev its engine. She braced herself, certain it was going to finish the deed, just as the WDR thugs had done to Charles Brandsmyth III.

She sat up and fumbled for the door handle. If the hulk pushed her car over the side, she wasn't going to go with it.

She opened the door to get out. The SUV was backing up, probably to get up speed. She leaped from the car, sprinted to the far side of the highway, and crouched behind a boulder.

Kate held her breath. One flash of the headlights in her direction, and they would spot her hiding place.

Her heart beat so hard she could hear it in her ears.

The SUV revved its engine, the accelerator floorboarded.

Kate squeezed her eyes shut, waiting for the crash of metal and glass as her Honda was pushed over the side.

But all was still.

The SUV had stopped. How close she didn't know. She was afraid to look.

Then she heard the engine backing away from her.

She forced her eyes open and peered out from behind the boulder. The SUV was out of sight, probably on the other side of the curve. Still waiting. Still planning to come in for the kill.

She shivered.

A flash of headlights in the distance caught her attention. A car coming from the opposite direction.

For one wild moment, she considered that the SUV had found a shortcut and doubled back to hit her from the other side.

No. The occupants of the SUV had probably seen the headlights and hightailed it out of there.

The snow was falling steadily. And so were Kate's tears. She stumbled back to the car, fell into the seat, started the engine, but was shaking too hard to press the accelerator. She turned off the ignition.

Then she bowed her head over the steering wheel.

The car she had seen earlier was closer now. She could hear the low hum of the engine, and from time to time, the flash of headlights shone through the trees.

She thought about waving down whoever it was for help. But she was certain that if she tried to exit the car again, her knees would buckle.

The vehicle stopped, and she heard the door open, then close. Footsteps approached.

She held her breath.

Chapter Twenty-Three

The crunch of footsteps moved closer. Kate squeezed her eyes closed and tried to breathe.

"Katie, is that you?" called a familiar voice.

Her eyes flew open. Paul was running toward her. He was fine. His Lexus was fine. Whatever car trouble he'd had must have been fixed.

Or she had been tricked.

"What happened? Why are you out here?"

She fell into his arms. "Oh, Paul," she said, and wept. He held her tight against his warm parka until she could speak. "Just another one of those ordinary days in the life of a minister's wife," she hiccuped and then told him what happened.

The Honda had suffered dents and scrapes, but no engine damage. The passenger side, where Kate had been forced against the protruding rocks, bore the brunt of the damage.

Paul assured her that there had been no accident and that the thugs from WDR had likely staged the whole thing. He turned the Honda around, then they drove down the mountain in tandem, Kate following Paul's Lexus.

He insisted they go home rather than to the sheriff's office. She didn't argue. All she could think of was a hot bath and a cup of hot chocolate by the fire.

Paul drew her bubble bath, then while she soaked, he made the call to the sheriff in Pine Ridge. He gave the sheriff the license number that Kate had had the presence of mind to write down after Paul's arrival. And he told him about the ghoulish gift left for Kate earlier that evening. Sheriff Roberts assured him they would do a thorough investigation, though he said it was almost a certainty that the same thugs that tried to run Kate off the road probably left the stuffed Chihuahua.

It wasn't until the house was quiet and Paul was in bed that she sat down by the fire and let the full impact of the experience sink in.

Kisses jumped up on her lap and settled down to get warm in her robe. Ruffles wandered in from the kitchen, where he'd no doubt been roaming around on the counter.

He jumped up to take his place on Kate's lap, saw the dog, and put his ears back.

Kisses whimpered, probably missing Renee, and Kate moved him to the crook of her arm to make room for Ruffles. The animals eyed each other warily, then slowly relaxed.

They both settled down, one purring, one snoring. And Kate's heart finally started to beat at a normal rhythm.

THE NEXT TWO WEEKS raced by in a blur. Just four days after the incident on the mountain, the two men in the SUV were caught, charged with harassment and attempted murder, then extradited to California where other charges were brought against them for the death of Charles Brandsmyth III. They were on the payroll of Worldwide Destination Resorts and worked in the computer-resources division, which made sense, Kate thought, because of the e-mail death threat. Though, as Skip explained, the computer-resources title was more a cover-up for their extracurricular activities than a nine-to-five job.

The *Chronicle* published several stories about the apprehension, complete with Kate's photograph and mention of her brave "confrontation" of the thugs when they tried to run her off the mountain road.

She told everyone who mentioned the article that there had been no confrontation. Quite the opposite; she was so scared, a pack of wolves running after her would have been a relief in comparison.

It didn't matter. She'd had her fifteen minutes of fame and had now become something of a local celebrity.

Renee called the day the first article was released to make sure Kate hadn't had Kisses with her on that wild mountain ride. Lester and LeRoy did the same, though why they would think she'd take a cat with her on a mountain drive was beyond her comprehension.

Just when things were getting back to normal, and the townspeople had moved on to other local news, a special edition was published in which it was reported that the two men, now in California, had agreed to name names at WDR in a plea bargain.

Charley and Clarence Brandsmyth, the lumber thieves, were apprehended in a Kentucky saloon after they bragged about the "caper" they'd been in on—stealing lumber from a church—and how a little old lady had tried to stop them single-handedly, coming at them wielding a flashlight.

Kate was sure that Renee would be insulted if she knew about the "little old lady" part in the police report. It was a blessing that the *Chronicle* didn't print the direct quote and only said it was due to her quick thinking that the criminals were apprehended.

But though WDR wanted the land, the company vehemently denied having anything to do with the church fire.

Which left a single clue: the baseball cap.

THE DAY BEFORE the pumpkin festival, Paul went fishing with Eli and Sam. Kate took Kisses by Renee's for a visit on her way to the deputy's office. The little dog was beside himself with joy as Renee scooped him into her arms.

Renee's eyes filled with tears, which she quickly brushed away.

Her mother was watching, and Kate thought she saw a softening in her expression. But she said, "Little umpkins schmumpkins, *hmmph.*"

Renee walked Kate to the car. "It won't be long," she said. "Mama's rather stubborn, but she's not heartless. I think she'll be okay with Kisses here eventually."

"What about the asthma?"

"Oh, that. She doesn't have asthma. It's congestive heart failure, but the first time the doctor mentioned it, she panicked. So now we're just calling it asthma."

"If there's any time I could just come by and take care of her, I'd be happy to. Give you some time away."

Renee started to come back with a snappy reply but

thought better of it—Kate could see it in her eyes—and said, "Thank you." Then she added, "Tomorrow, if there was a way . . ."

"I'll make sure there is. You can't miss the festival." Kate smiled. "Especially that pie-baking contest."

As usual, Skip was at the front desk at the office. It appeared that no matter how hard he tried, because of the mistakes he had made at the fire, the sheriff was reluctant to assign him to fieldwork again. The only positive outcome was that Skip was available, and willing, to discuss the case with Kate. They were forging a partnership of sorts, which was beneficial to them both.

"So far, the WDR investigation hasn't made any connection with the fire," he said.

"They may not want to divulge any more than they already have. But you'd think if there's a plea bargain, they would come clean about every detail."

"I don't think they're connected," he said.

"Then we're back to square one. Who did it?"

"Someone else with a grudge against the church," Skip said, shrugging. "Or against God."

"That's been my husband's theory from the beginning," Kate said.

"He may be right."

When Kate arrived home, Paul was just coming back from his fishing trip. He exited the backseat of Sam's vehicle and held up a string of pan-sized trout, looking tired but happy.

"I guess I know what you want for dinner tonight," she said, wrapping her arm around his waist.

He doffed his baseball cap, waved to Sam and Eli as they drove off, and then handed it to Kate. As he headed to the stationary tub in the garage to clean the fish, Kate took his cap in the house to hang in the coat closet.

She turned the cap over in her hands and lifted it toward the hook. Then she stopped, frowning, as the iridescent logo caught her attention.

"Oh no," she whispered. "Oh no."

When Paul came in the house a few minutes later, she was still holding his baseball cap.

"Honey, are you all right? You look like you've seen a ghost."

"I know who started the fire," she said.

Chapter Twenty-Four

After weeks of preparation, the first annual pumpkin festival was ready to begin.

The day of the opening, Kate woke before dawn, as usual. She pulled back the living-room drapes and looked out. The weather forecast had called for clear skies, and though an almost imperceptible pale violet light announced the coming dawn, it promised to be a perfect Indian-summer day.

Paul had worked on his pumpkin grits the night before, and she pulled the containers out of the refrigerator.

Though she missed Ruffles, she was glad he had gone home to the Philpott brothers and their mother, Enid, who was recovering nicely after her gall-bladder surgery. Otherwise, the grits wouldn't have been safe.

During Ruffles' stay, Kate learned early on to keep everything on the kitchen counter covered, not just with cellophane wrap or foil—the cat could eat his way through either—but with a heavy-glass or plastic-snap lid. She found he loved lasagna almost as much as he loved Paul's five-alarm chili. But his all-time favorite was Paul's grilled chicken with a sage and rosemary rub.

The animal had an iron stomach and never seemed to get full.

At her feet, Kisses sat looking up at Kate with his soulful gaze, his tiny tail thumping on the floor.

"Okay, little umpkins, what'll it be? Maple tree or breakfast first?"

She knew better than to ask. The maple was a do-or-die sort of thing. She grabbed a sweater and the leash and headed to the door.

The phone was ringing when she stepped back inside. Paul was in the shower, so she ran to pick up the phone. There were a million and one things to do before they left for the festival, and she was certain it would be LuAnne or Livvy on the phone.

"Mrs. Hanlon?" said a very weak voice.

"Yes, this is Mrs. Hanlon."

"This is Renee's mother, Caroline Beauregard Johnston."

"Oh yes, of course. Is everything all right?"

"Why wouldn't it be?"

Kate sighed and tried a different question. "How are you this morning?"

"Fair to middlin', I suppose, for an old lady."

Kate waited, but the woman didn't go on.

"It looks like it will be a beautiful day for our pumpkin festival. I'm hoping Renee will be able to get away. We've got someone lined up to come over and visit with you for a little while."

"I don't like strangers. Don't warm up to them easily, if you know what I mean."

"He's no stranger. He's my husband, and he's looking forward to it."

"Oh, the preacher?" Her tune changed. She sounded delighted. "Really?"

"Yes."

"Nothing I like better than a good old-fashioned talk about theological things. I hope he's ready for some fire-and-brimstone talk."

Kate stifled a smile. "Yes, I'm sure he will be."

"The reason I called is because Renee is fit to be tied over the idea she might not win the pumpkin-pie contest. She was up all night baking one pumpkin pie after another to get the perfect pie. She's very competitive, you know."

"How can I help?" For the life of her, Kate couldn't figure out why Caroline had called.

"I just hate seeing her so unhappy, especially after trying so hard to bake the perfect pie. I called because I know how upset she'll be if she doesn't win, and I'd like for you to bring that yippy little dog home after the doin's."

Kate smiled. "Of course. I can't think of anything I'd rather do."

PARKING WAS LIMITED DOWNTOWN, so Paul and Kate got an early start and walked to the festival. When they reached Main Street, they stood for a moment, looking at each other in astonishment, then back to what had been transformed into a pumpkin fairyland.

Tiny orange lights shaped like pumpkins were strung up

and down both sides of the street, along storefront rooflines, and window frames. Bales of hay, decorative haystacks, and fresh-cut real pumpkins were strategically placed on the sidewalk. It was pretty now; it would be utterly magical at night.

Canvas booths lined the street. Even from a short distance away, Kate could make out the booths filled with candles, wood carvings, paintings by local artists, needlework, and stained glass for sale. And, just as LuAnne promised, there were also painted saws with pastoral scenes of Tennessee's hill country. Booths selling all kinds of food were at the far end of the street, and Faith Briar Church had its own little booth across from the Mercantile, selling treats and crafts donated by church members, including Kate's stained-glass lamp.

In the distance, the band was warming up. Strains of "Seventy-six Trombones" drifted toward them as they made their way along Main Street, visiting with parishioners and friends along the way.

The parade was scheduled to open the festival. The band would march first, followed by Mayor Lawton Briddle and his wife, Lucy Mae, in an orange VW Bug. Riders on Arabian horses would follow, then all the children, who were dressed like pumpkins.

As people gathered along the parade route, Kate took in the crowd. There had to be a couple thousand people here already, and more were pouring in. She recognized a few, but most were strangers. Yet they were all here because of Faith Briar.

She whispered to Paul, "Think of it, honey. This all began because one person had the seed of an idea."

"LuAnne Matthews."

"Yes. And just look what grew from her idea."

Paul nodded, his eyes on the people around them. "And all the rest . . ." He turned, smiling as if in wonder. "Some are from other denominations, other towns, or other counties. Yet they've all come to help us with the sticks and mortar we need to rebuild. It's almost overwhelming."

The band started to play, and the crowd fell silent as it rounded the corner. It was impressive, every member dressed in navy blue and gold, marching in step, swinging gloved hands.

Eli came up to stand beside Kate as the band neared. It stopped in front of where they were standing to do some fancy footwork while playing "When the Saints Go Marching In."

Eli smiled. "I love parades," he said. They watched in silence for a moment, then he slowly turned to her. "So did Diedre."

It was the first time Eli had mentioned her name, and his eyes watered behind his thick glasses.

"You still miss her," she said softly.

He nodded. "I'll never stop loving her. We were supposed to get married a few months ago."

"I know."

"Then the cancer hit." He was watching the band while he talked. "And everything changed."

The band did a few more crisp turns while the majorette tossed her baton higher and higher, catching it behind her back and under her leg, then tossing it up in the air again. The band finished the song and marched on by.

THE MORNING SPED BY. Joe Tucker spotted Kate and Paul at the Faith Briar booth and reminded them to drop by the booth selling his hand-carved walking sticks. Others stopped at the table to visit—Betty Anderson, the Pippins, and Sam Gorman. The excitement was contagious. Betty said she'd heard they had made thousands of dollars, and it wasn't even noon.

The group was just leaving to have a look at Joe's walking sticks when Sam, MC for the day, excused himself to go to the podium. A few minutes later, his booming baritone announced the upcoming events.

"Come one, come all," he called out. "Find out who will be crowned Little Miss Pumpkin and Little Mister Pumpkin at the first annual Copper Mill pumpkin festival. The contest begins in exactly ninety minutes."

Paul gave Kate a quick kiss, then left to walk to Renee's to sit with her mother.

LuAnne sidled over to Kate, eating orange cotton candy.

"Pumpkin flavor, darlin'," LuAnne said. "Want a bite?" She broke off a piece and stuffed it in Kate's mouth.

"*Hmm*," Kate said. "Tastes like stale cinnamon-and-nutmeg-flavored bubble gum."

"Darlin', you don't know what's good eatin' at one of these affairs." She laughed. "Hey, I'm on my way to see who won the pumpkin-pie contest. Want to come along?"

Kate took off her apron and headed across the street to the park where the stage and bleachers had been set up.

People were drifting over to take their seats in the audience, and the contestants were hovering near the stage.

There were kids in pumpkin costumes of every shape and size. Off to one side, judges were sampling the pumpkin-pie entries.

Kate looked around for Renee, but when she didn't see her, she sat down next to LuAnne. "Have you seen Renee?"

"No, I haven't."

"Paul's staying with her mother so Renee could get away."

Kate checked her watch, then scanned the crowd again.

Someone tapped her on the shoulder, and she turned. It was Renee, wringing her hands and looking very nervous. "Have they started yet?"

"Partway through, I think."

"I brought my pie over early this morning. Wanted it to be the first they tried so the memory of that bite would transcend all the others." She paused, frowning. "You two didn't enter, did you?"

LuAnne laughed. "Darlin', I can serve up pies till the cows come home, but I wouldn't know the first thing about makin' one from scratch."

"My mind's been preoccupied," Kate said.

Renee shot her a knowing look. "Having to do with BOLO?"

Kate grinned. "'Be on the lookout.' Nothing describes my preoccupation better."

Children in pumpkin costumes paraded through the area, followed by the Copper Mill High School marching-band majorette performing to the beat of snare and bass drums.

A drumroll followed as one of the judges walked to center stage. Portly and balding, Willy Bergen, owner of Willy's Bait and Tackle, looked like a man who knew his way around a pumpkin pie. He cleared his throat into the mic and announced, "Third runner-up: Trudy Johnson!" A small blonde woman smiled and walked to the stage to accept the ribbon Willy was holding out.

"Second runner-up: Candace Kent!" The crowd went wild, clapping and cheering.

Another drumroll preceded the announcement of the first runner-up: "Renee Lambert!"

Kate shot a glance at Renee, who looked like a thunder-cloud, lips tight, arms crossed in front of her chest. She clearly didn't like being runner-up, but she reluctantly went to the stage and let Willy pin a ribbon on her.

Another drumroll sounded, this time longer and louder. Then Willy called out, "Our first-place winner of the most delicious pumpkin pie in all of Tennessee is..." Another drumroll interrupted him, so he shouted louder than before: "Betty Anderson!"

The crowd clapped and cheered, then surged forward to buy tastes—fifty cents a spoonful—of the winning pies, and lighthearted chaos reigned.

Afterward, Kate looked everywhere for Renee to congratulate her, but she had disappeared. She finally gave up and went back to work in the Faith Briar booth.

Paul found her there.

"Renee must have gone home immediately after the contest," Kate said.

He nodded. "She didn't seem too happy."

"Renee doesn't strike me as the kind of person who likes to be runner-up to anybody for anything."

"She said the only reason Betty Anderson won was

because she gave the judges free hairdos. She plans to boy-
cott all future festivals plus spread the word that the judges
are biased."

"She put her all into this, Paul. Her mother said she was
up all night baking pies, trying to find the perfect recipe. Was
she okay when you left?"

"She was her usual incorrigible self, ranting on and on,
but I could see how devastated she was deep down. She was
having a hard time holding back her tears."

Chapter Twenty-Five

After Paul left to check out the barbecue stand, Kate headed to the pumpkin weigh-in, enjoying a hot dog with all the fixin's on the way. She didn't even like hot dogs and couldn't understand why they tasted so good at a ball game or fair, or in this case, a pumpkin festival. She was glad she talked LuAnne out of ordering pumpkin-apple sausages for a rather different tasting hot dog.

Up ahead, she spotted Eli pushing a wheelbarrow into a large tent where the pumpkins were kept before they were judged.

She followed him inside.

The tent was as big as a barn, with hundreds of pumpkins of all sizes scattered around on a hay-covered floor.

Eli was on the far side of the tent by a mound of small pumpkins, loading them into the wheelbarrow. He turned when he heard the crunch of her footsteps in the hay.

She stared at him, a million thoughts running through her head.

He spoke first. "You've figured it out, haven't you?"

She nodded.

"I saw it in your face at the parade." Eli let his gaze drift away from hers. "It was a fantasy, I suppose, but I had hoped you and Pastor Paul would never find out."

She finally found her voice. "The day of the fire was your wedding day, wasn't it?"

He stared at her, then swallowed hard and said, "How did you know?"

"I didn't. At least until you talked about it this morning. Then the pieces began to fit together. I already knew about the baseball cap."

He frowned. "What cap?"

"Jed Brawley saw you run from the church that morning. But all he recognized was the iridescent logo on the front of your hat. He said it looked like a pirate." She paused. "Or, more accurately, a buccaneer."

Eli's quick intake of breath was audible. "And Pastor Paul has one like it. I've seen it."

"He wore it fishing yesterday. It has the official logo of the East Tennessee State Buccaneers, your alma mater, and Paul's."

"The fire was an accident." He swept back his shock of blond hair. His face was pale, and his brown eyes seemed larger than ever behind his tortoiseshell glasses.

"I figured that, Eli." She kept her voice low, though truth be told, her sadness for him, for them all, made it difficult to speak.

"Diedre and I had planned it for years, then cancer took her. I was inconsolable. She was everything to me."

Kate took a step toward him, but he backed away. "Please, stay away from me."

She held up a hand to calm him. "It's all right. Go on."

"I went into the sanctuary to yell at God, to tell him everything I'd kept pent up for all those weeks and months. Something about the place was comforting, maybe a sense of holiness, or maybe the memories of being there with my grandparents when I was a little kid.

"For a long time, I didn't do anything. I just stared up at the cross. Then I sat down in the first pew and started talking to God. I spewed out my bitter story, I railed on and on, and I cried until I had no more tears left to cry.

"And then, in the stillness, I felt his touch. His forgiveness. His mercy."

Eli fell silent for a moment. Outside the tent, the sounds of the festival went on, the laughter of little children, the blare of Sam's voice over the PA system announcing the winner of some event, and somewhere in the distance, the band played "Way Down upon the Sewanee River."

"When it was over," Eli said finally, "I was exhausted. I'd been staying up day and night, unable to sleep because of my grief. I was emotionally wrung out. I fell asleep, right there in front of the altar."

"That still doesn't explain how the fire started," Kate said.

"I lit a candle. The flame was to remind me of God's refining fire. I wanted to start over fresh. I wanted to be rid of the bitterness and hatred.

"When I fell asleep, I must have knocked it somehow." He shrugged. "However it happened, the candle fell over and caught the altar cloth on fire. That's when I woke up and tried for a few minutes to put it out. But it spread so quickly, I ran away like the coward I am."

"You've got to tell Sheriff Roberts."

He shook his head. "Who's gonna believe me?"

"I do."

"I can't go to jail. You don't understand. I would die in jail. I've told you how I feel about being outdoors. Working in the shop is bad enough, but if I was locked up . . . I-I wouldn't survive. If I don't tell, then I don't have to worry about it. Everything's cool." His expression didn't match his cavalier words.

"You're weighed down with guilt, Eli. You will be until the day you die unless you tell what happened."

"I can't," he said and dropped his head in his hands.

"Come with me, Eli. I'll go with you." She took a few steps toward him.

He shook his head and backed away from her. "I tried to make up for what I did—all the plans, the construction, all that was to try to pay back what I'd taken from you." He was crying now. "But it still wasn't enough."

"I know. But you need to understand that none of this takes away from the gift you've given us—all you've done. Or your friendship with Pastor Paul and me. That will never change, no matter what happens."

He was still shaking his head. "I can't, I'm sorry." He started for the door.

Skip Spencer stepped out of the shadows. "Oh no, you don't," he said solemnly. "You're coming with me."

Skip shot Kate a look that surprised her. She thought he might be proud of his first real arrest. But his freckled face showed only sadness.

The two walked out of the tent together, and Kate sat down on a hay bale and cried.

Chapter Twenty-Six

The weather turned cold by the end of November, and by Christmas Eve, light snow was falling on Copper Mill. Snow blanketed the ground and clung to the branches of the evergreens, giving the town the look of a winter fairyland.

It was three thirty in the afternoon, and Paul and Kate were getting ready to leave for the four o'clock Christmas Eve service at the church.

At the church. What a blessing those three little words brought to Kate. For too long everyone had referred to it as "the property" or "the burn site" or "the building site."

The church wasn't finished. Far from it. There were Sunday-school classrooms to build and the fellowship hall to complete downstairs. But the foundation was done, the framing up, the roof on, and most of the wallboard nailed into place. Best of all, the money from the pumpkin festival had allowed them to build the new steeple, which rose majestically into the air with its historic bell in place.

Paul helped Kate into her coat, then reached for his own. They stood for a moment in the entry hall, looking toward the

living room. A garland with twinkling lights stretched across
the mantel and cascaded down from either end. A Christmas
tree with thousands of lights stood tall and proud and fragrant
by the piano. Handmade ornaments collected through the
years graced its branches.

"What a transformation," Paul said. "Who would believe
it's the same room?"

"It's just like our hearts," she said softly. "Transformed."

He looked down at her. "Are you still homesick?"

"Sometimes, but not as often. This place—and I don't
mean just the parsonage—feels like home now. I can't imagine
ever leaving."

"You've done a lot for the community, Kate, and they've
embraced you because of it. They're still talking about how
you uncovered the crooks at WDR. It wouldn't have happened if you hadn't looked into it."

Kate smiled. She *was* proud of the outcome. She had
heard from Sybil Hudson that plans for the hotel had been
scaled down to fit the property WDR already owned, but they
still planned to go through with the upscale renovation. The
new management team had approached Sybil about becoming general manager of the hotel and spa once it was up and
running. She was considering it.

"We've been blessed," Kate said, "from the first day we
arrived—even though it seemed like the worst possible cir-
cumstance to find ourselves in."

"Any regrets?"

"Not a one. How about you?"

A half smile played at the corner of his mouth. "I've had

little twinges, but not many. The worst was watching my Lexus go at the auction."

"At least it was bought by someone in Pine Ridge, so you don't have to see it all the time. And now you've got Joe Tucker's old pickup truck to rattle around in. Don't you think it's a bit more, well, 'you'?"

Paul laughed. "Actually, I do." He checked his watch. "We'd better go."

"The minister can't be late."

"Neither can the minister's wife."

DUSK WAS FALLING as they entered the unfinished church. Kate took her place in one of the folding chairs and watched as the rest of the congregation entered. There was a hush of wonder when, for the first time since the fire, people walked into their church.

LuAnne came in with Lester and LeRoy and their mother, Enid. Livvy, Danny, and their boys walked down the center aisle and sat in the row in front of Kate. Next came Renee, pushing her mother in a wheelchair. Wonder of wonders, Kisses was sitting on Caroline's lap, ears up, big eyes bright.

Kate smiled as others entered, surprised that after only four months, they had become so dear to her. By four o'clock, the sanctuary was packed.

Before Paul stood to open the service, there was a slight stir in the back of the sanctuary.

Kate turned around. Eli Weston and Jed Packer entered together, caught her eye, and sidled into her row of folding chairs. Jed gave her a wink, and Eli gave her a hug before sitting down. The two had become good friends, having taken on the job of designing the expanded kitchen and the fellowship hall. It was part of Eli's commitment to community service as handed down by the judge, but it was also his labor of love.

Paul opened the service with prayer, then the children performed "Little Drummer Boy" and "Away in a Manger."

Paul's sermon was taken from Isaiah 61, which had been so comforting during the weeks of grief after the fire. Now it took on even greater meaning, because, as Paul pointed out, the words foretold the role of the coming Savior: "He was sent to . . . bring good news to the poor . . . comfort the brokenhearted . . . announce that captives will be released and prisoners freed . . . and to all who mourn, he will give beauty for ashes, joy instead of mourning.

"He is here, with us now, the newborn King," Paul said at the sermon's conclusion. "He has come to us just as surely as he came to the manger two thousand years ago.

"He has given us beauty for ashes . . ." He looked around at the unfinished room, smiling, "But it's not what you think. It's not the beauty of the building that's rising out of the ashes. No, my friends, it's the beauty in each one of you. Your strength and courage, your joy, your grace . . . these too rose from the ashes. We have truly been refined, and that, my friends, is true beauty. That is what we celebrate today."

At the end of his sermon, Paul announced that the service would continue outdoors in candlelight, as they dedicated the newly finished steeple and installed bell.

With the congregation softly singing "Silent Night," they all filed outside, each one holding a candle.

As Kate followed the others, she fingered the small folded piece of paper in her coat pocket. There had been a drawing the Sunday before to choose the one who would ring the bell for the first time since the fire. Her name had been chosen, and she had anticipated this moment all week.

The snow continued to fall as the congregation clustered together. Faces glowed in the candlelight, and when Paul switched on the spotlight, the crowd gasped. The old bell looked strong and sure and beautiful in its new tower, the steeple pointing into the snowy heavens.

Kate glanced at Renee, who stood off to one side, with her mother in the wheelchair. She had taken off her coat to cover her mother's lap, and she stood shivering in the snowy cold.

But it was as if she didn't even notice. There was a look on her face that Kate had never seen before. All pretense, all bitterness, all snootiness was gone. All that was left was pure awe.

Paul cleared his throat to announce that Kate had been chosen to ring the bell, but she signaled him with a slight shake of the head.

He knew her well and waited.

Kate walked over to Renee. "You're the one, Renee," she whispered. "Did you know that you've been chosen to ring that beautiful bell?"

The look on Renee's face was priceless. She practically flew to the base of the steeple, where Paul waited to help her pull the ropes.

As the bell tolled, Sam started to sing "On Holy Ground." One by one, the others joined in. Kate remembered the tears that fell the first time Sam played the song in her living room the Sunday after the fire.

Now, voices were lifted in praise and thanksgiving, and the beloved candlelit faces of the Faith Briar congregation were filled with joy.

As the last toll of the bell echoed across the snowy landscape, Kate couldn't stop smiling. God had brought them to this place for such a time as this. Oh yes, he had!

About the Author

DIANE NOBLE is the award-winning author of *The Butterfly Farm* and nearly two dozen other published works—mysteries, romantic suspense, historical fiction, and non-fiction books for women, including three devotionals and an empty nest survival guide. Diane is a three-time recipient of the Silver Angel Award for Media Excellence and a double finalist for RWA's prestigious RITA award for Best Inspirational Fiction. Diane makes her home in Southern California with husband Tom and their two cats. You can stop by Diane's Web site at www.dianenoble.com to catch up on the latest about her books, favorite recipes, crochet patterns, and much more.

A Note from the Editors

THIS ORIGINAL BOOK was created by the Books and Inspirational Media Division of Guideposts, the world's leading inspirational publisher. Founded in 1945 by Dr. Norman Vincent Peale and his wife Ruth Stafford Peale, Guideposts helps people from all walks of life achieve their maximum personal and spiritual potential. Guideposts is committed to communicating positive, faith-filled principles for people everywhere to use in successful daily living.

Our publications include award-winning magazines like *Guideposts*, *Angels on Earth* and *Positive Thinking*, best-selling books, and outreach services that demonstrate what can happen when faith and positive thinking are applied in day-to-day life.

For more information, visit us online at www .guideposts.org, call (800) 431-2344 or write Guideposts, 39 Seminary Hill Road, Carmel, New York 10512.